"You kissed me, but it didn't mean anything to you."

Robert's expression gave nothing away. "Do you honestly believe what you're saying?"

"Yes ... yes, I do. Oh, I expect you found those kisses pleasant enough. But they're just part of you railroading your way into my life. You want to take my restaurant, and you want to take a few kisses along the way, too ... and afterward you plan to go barreling off to some new goal."

When Robert didn't respond, Gwen glared at him defiantly. "You're not going to get the restaurant. I'm going to give you one humdinger of a battle. And no more kisses! You got that? No more kisses."

"No more," he repeated solemnly. Then he cupped her face with both hands, smiled at her and planted a firm, no-nonsense kiss on her mouth. He stepped back. "We'll have none of that, Gwennie."

Ellen James has wanted a writing career ever since she won a national short-story contest when she was in high school. *Home For Christmas* is Ellen's seventh Harlequin Romance novel. She and her husband, both writers, love to travel. They also share an interest in wildlife photography and American history.

Books by Ellen James

HARLEQUIN ROMANCE
3052—HOME FOR LOVE
3069—THE TURQUOISE HEART
3118—TWO AGAINST LOVE
3154—LOVE'S HARBOR
3202—LOVE YOUR ENEMY
3254—GROWING ATTRACTION

HOME FOR CHRISTMAS
Ellen James

Harlequin Books

TORONTO • NEW YORK • LONDON
AMSTERDAM • PARIS • SYDNEY • HAMBURG
STOCKHOLM • ATHENS • TOKYO • MILAN
MADRID • WARSAW • BUDAPEST • AUCKLAND

ISBN 0-373-03291-9

HOME FOR CHRISTMAS

CHAPTER ONE

EVEN AT CHRISTMAS! Yet another offer from that infuriating man's lawyers. Gwen couldn't believe she was being hounded now, in the middle of the holiday season. She spread the letter out on one of the kitchen counters and read it over again. The lawyers were proposing a bigger sum than ever to buy her share of Pop's Restaurant. But she'd already turned them down plenty of times. What made them think more money could sway her?

She was tempted to crumple up the letter and toss it into the trash, just as she'd done with all the others. But then she began folding the single sheet of paper. A crease here, another crease there, a tuck and then a twist—perfect. Apparently she hadn't lost her talent for making paper airplanes. She launched this new model, watching as it floated across the kitchen. Then her plane took a nosedive—landing right at the feet of a dark-haired man who'd appeared in the doorway.

"Do you have a pilot's license for this thing?" The man bent down, picked up the airplane and regarded it critically.

"Hey, I'm practically a professional," Gwen said. "I used to make paper planes all the time for my kid sisters."

The man shook his head. "We're talking major wind-shear problems here." Quickly he added a few new folds to the plane, turning it into a more streamlined version. Taking aim, he sent it whizzing back toward Gwen. It flew fast and trim now, not even a hint of a wobble to its wings. The landing alone was impressive: the plane glided smoothly over the counter and slowed to a halt in front of Gwen.

She prodded the airplane with one finger. "Flashy. Very flashy." She surveyed the man. "I don't suppose you're my new produce supplier. I'm awfully low on mushrooms."

He looked faintly amused. "No. I'm not in produce." He didn't say anything more, just stood there in the doorway, examining the kitchen with a quizzical thoroughness, rather like an archaeologist who's just discovered the remnants of an ancient civilization. Gwen's half-built gingerbread house resting on the counter, her wreaths of red chili peppers adorning the walls, her well-thumbed cookbooks piled haphazardly on a shelf—the man studied everything with a thoughtful frown. Goodness, no one else had ever seemed quite so interested in the restaurant's homey and cluttered little kitchen.

Gwen was intrigued by the man, despite the way he'd commandeered her airplane. People fascinated Gwen, all shapes and sizes of people. She'd look at them and try to picture the many details of their lives. Now she propped her elbows on the counter and gave this man a judicial once-over.

He was tall and broad of shoulder, his head brushing the evergreen boughs that hung from the door lintel. His wavy hair was so dark it reminded Gwen of the color of ripe black currants. His eyes, however, were an unusual shade of light brown. Golden hazel, that's what they were, startling in contrast to the dark eyebrows furrowed above them.

He had the commanding air of a successful businessman—but there was a restlessness about him that Gwen couldn't quite define. Maybe it was because he wasn't dressed like a businessman. Was he an entrepreneur of some sort? A maverick, no matter what he did for a living, evidenced by the way he'd paired that expensive jacket with his well-worn jeans.

"You can't be a customer for lunch," she said. "It's much too early. But let me guess. You own a restaurant-equipment firm, and you're here to convince me I need a new cheese grater."

"Keep guessing."

"Hmm...I know. You want me to cater a party and serve dozens and dozens of my Florentine chicken rolls."

"Wrong again, Ms. Ferris." The man appeared to have no interest at all in Gwen's Florentine chicken rolls.

"I give up. You seem to know who I am, but who are you? Can I help you with something?"

He stared at her intently. "You can help me a lot, Ms. Gwendolyn Ferris. You can agree to sell your half of the restaurant to me."

Gwen straightened. "You're Robert Beltramo?"

"That's me."

So this was the man whose lawyers had been driving her nuts the past few months, trying to disrupt her entire life. She wasn't happy to see him, not happy at all. She retied her apron with a good yank on the strings, then threw the paper airplane back toward him. She missed her mark and watched with wry satisfaction as the plane landed in a bowl of Sicilian cake batter.

"That's from you, actually," she said. "It's the latest letter I've received from your lawyers. You've had them harassing me day and night. I told them I wouldn't sell. And I'm telling you the same thing."

He pulled the airplane out of the batter and unfolded its sticky flaps. "You've given new meaning to the concept of airmail, Gwendolyn. But I have good lawyers, and they've made you a very generous offer. What's the holdup?"

Gwen took a deep breath. She'd suspected that sooner or later this face-to-face confrontation with Robert Beltramo would come. She'd tried to prepare herself for it, and she had her arguments well laid out.

"I worked several years for your father before I bought half of the restaurant from him. We were negotiating so I could buy the rest of the place. But then...his health deteriorated so quickly there wasn't any time." Gwen struggled to keep her voice carefully emotionless and businesslike. She'd loved crusty old Pop Beltramo, and his death had greatly saddened her. "Anyway, Pop never talked about you. I didn't even know until after he died that he had a son, or that he'd left you his half of the restaurant in his will. It was all very surprising and mysterious."

The vigorous lines of Robert's face seemed to tighten. "My father didn't talk about me? Not once?"

"No, I'm afraid he didn't." Gwen saw a flash of bitterness in Robert's eyes, perhaps even pain. But it was obvious he didn't want her to see these emotions, and his frown intensified. He gave the handle of the pasta machine an aggressive crank.

The mystery surrounding Robert Beltramo had just deepened for Gwen. What had happened between him and Pop? She knew Pop had been a difficult, ill-tempered man, stubborn and proud. But with Gwen he had shown a gruff tenderness, treating her like a daughter. What could have kept him from mentioning his own son all those years? The only information Gwen had ever been able to get out of Pop was that he'd lost his wife when he was quite young. Beyond that he'd refused to talk about his family.

The restlessness Gwen had sensed in Robert seemed to erupt. He began prowling around the kitchen, acting for all the world like a belligerent health inspector. He nudged the sprigs of holly tucked everywhere in odd places—next to the salt box, on top of the spice rack, poking out from underneath a stack of china plates. He popped the lids off Gwen's Christmas tins and peered inside them. He picked up bottles of olive oil and cooking wine, only to set them down again with a clatter. Then he gestured at the pots and pans cluttering the sink, the eggplants and onions and tomatoes strewn across one counter, the confectioners' sugar dusting the floor.

"This place is one hell of a mess. Looks like a tornado hit in here." Now his gaze centered on Gwen. He examined her as if she were just one more kitchen disaster that needed mopping up. She flushed. If she'd known Robert Beltramo was going to show up like this, out of nowhere, she would've tried for a little sophistication today. As it was, this morning she'd merely tossed on her favorite clothes: a cotton polo shirt the exact same blue-gray as her eyes, and her oldest and coziest jeans, the ones with holes in the pockets so she was always losing her change. She'd pulled her tawny hair into a simple ponytail so it would be out of her way while she cooked. However, she had taken the time to choose something from her hodge-podge of antique jewelry: a porcelain miniature, which dangled from her neck by a blue silk ribbon. Gwen loved old jewelry—especially Victorian—and couldn't resist wearing hints of the past, even when they were at odds with the casual clothes she favored. Unfortunately, that was how she felt right now under Robert Beltramo's gaze—thoroughly at odds. She fingered her pendant, but most of Robert's attention seemed focused on the voluminous apron she wore. Gwen glanced down, remembering belatedly that the apron was smeared with splats of dried anchovy paste and tomato sauce.

"Lord. You look like you danced the tango with a pizza," Robert said. "What kind of operation are you running here, anyway?"

Gwen's flush deepened. "A good chef always gets involved with her food. And I *am* a good chef, Mr. Beltramo. This restaurant is thriving even though your father's gone. It'll continue to thrive if you leave it in my hands where it belongs. It so happens my own lawyer made a decent offer to buy your share of the place. Why don't you just agree to that? Go back to

New York where you belong. You probably don't even know anything about the restaurant business.''

Robert crossed the kitchen and flipped up the breadboard that had been cleverly hinged into one of the counters. He pointed to the jagged initials etched on the underside of the board, in the very back corner: R.B.

''Mine,'' he said. ''Carved when I was nine years old and first started working in this place. I went right on working here until I left for college. You can bet I know the business.''

Gwen came closer. She prided herself on a thorough acquaintance with this kitchen, but she'd never noticed those initials before. She felt uncomfortable, and she wondered what other secrets she'd missed.

Now she hurried over to the ovens and pulled out a loaf of her Italian sweet bread. She'd almost let it burn, distracted as she was by Robert's presence. ''I wasn't aware you'd worked here at all,'' she said.

''If my father never talked about me, I suppose you wouldn't know.'' His tone was sardonic, but there was a tenseness underneath. And, as if he needed to be on the move again, he circled the kitchen one more time, pausing in front of the battered old dishwashing machine. ''So this monster's still around,'' he murmured. ''That's how I used to think of it. A monster swallowing up dishes—and swallowing up all my time, all those after-school hours when I wanted to be shooting baskets, not scrubbing pots.''

He wandered to the window, decorated now with frolicking reindeer and lacy snowflakes. Gwen loved those silvery flakes sparkling on the windowpane;

tropical San Antonio simply wasn't the place for real snow. Robert, however, didn't seem to appreciate the holiday motif.

"Damn fool stuff," he muttered, angling his head so he could see out between a pair of reindeer antlers. He gazed at the lush greenery that surrounded Pop's Restaurant—banana trees, palms, wild hibiscus. The dark green water of the San Antonio River flowed by, mellow in the December sunlight. Passers-by thronged among all the shops and other restaurants lining the River Walk. After a moment Robert spoke in a low voice, as if to himself.

"I used to stare out this window and plot my escape. Used to tell myself I'd just leave one morning and never come back. The old man would be yelling at me, and I wouldn't even listen. In my head I'd be a thousand miles away from here..." His voice died, and a silence stretched out. Gwen began slicing an eggplant, the whisper of her knife the only sound in the room. After years in the restaurant business, she was a good listener. She knew how to let a silence linger. She gave her customers delicious food, and she also offered a sympathetic ear to their hopes and dreams and problems. She liked listening to people almost as much as she liked feeding them. But now Robert swiveled away from the window and scowled at her as if she'd tricked him into saying too much, or perhaps remembering too much.

"I don't know how the hell we got off the subject."

Gwen sliced another eggplant. "I think we're right on the subject. From the sound of things, you hated this place when you were growing up. You couldn't wait to get away. And according to your lawyers, you've made it really big in advertising. Why on earth do you want to run a restaurant all of a sudden—especially a restaurant you seem to despise?''

Robert rubbed the back of his neck, his brow furrowing more deeply. Gwen's question seemed to make him uneasy.

"Things change," he muttered. "My father died, and I started to feel like something was missing. Look, I'm here. That's all that matters."

"I still don't understand why you want to come back after all the success you've achieved in New York."

"It's an old tradition, coming home for the holidays," he said mockingly. "And maybe I got an invitation to come back—from my own father. He left me half this place in his will. Yep, that's an invitation if I ever heard of one."

Again, the sarcasm in his voice seemed to hide some deeper emotion. Gwen began slicing a zucchini. "I've already tried to tell you. Pop wanted to sell the rest of the place to me. We were working things out when he got sick.... Listen, I don't know what happened between the two of you. But I do know Pop wanted me to keep running his restaurant after he was gone. You should respect his wishes."

Robert looked grim and unyielding. "The only thing that counts is that he didn't change his will. He left me an inheritance, and I'm here to claim it."

Gwen's knife was moving faster now. She decimated the zucchini and started on the tomatoes. "I was your father's partner," she declared. "He trusted me to keep his memory alive—to keep this place going the way he would've wanted."

"You keep talking about all these plans between you and my father. But you didn't even show up at his funeral."

Gwen stiffened. "Pop hated funerals. He used to say they were a bunch of sentimental hooey. He didn't want one for himself. He made that very clear to me. But after he died—and your lawyers started hounding me—I found out you were going to take charge of all the arrangements. It was out of my control—out of Pop's control. So I held my own private memorial service, no sentimental hooey allowed, just the way he wanted it."

Robert gave a curt shrug. "It turned out to be a joke, my dad's funeral. No one there but me and the mortuary director. Think my father would've appreciated the humor in that?"

Gwen listened to the trace of bitter irony in Robert's voice when he spoke about his father. But now Robert's impatience was obviously growing. He glanced around the kitchen again.

"Forget the past," he said brusquely. "It's the future I want to think about. When I take over this place, I'll finally have a chance to change things around here. I can turn the restaurant into a profitable enterprise, instead of a bumbling little business."

Gwen stared at him in dismay. "This place is fine just the way it is. It doesn't need to change. It has a warm friendly atmosphere where people can relax and eat fettuccine and remember your dad. That's the legacy he wanted to leave."

"Get real, Gwendolyn. The old guy was a grouch and never tried to be chummy with his customers. He didn't leave anybody behind to sit around and toast his memory with eggnog."

This was too close to the truth, but Gwen knew she'd seen something more in Pop. Maybe no one else had been able to see it, but *she* had. "At heart your father was...convivial. Or at least he wanted to be a convivial person. He just needed the proper encouragement."

Robert's expression was highly skeptical. He watched Gwen work away with her knife.

"You're going to chop off your fingers," he said. "Here, let me show you the right way to do that." He shrugged out of his jacket and rolled up his sleeves. Before Gwen could protest, he took hold of her knife and demonstrated his own slicing technique. "Okay. First cut off the stem, then rotate the tomato like this. Always chop away from your fingers... Hey, I haven't lost my touch. What do you know? Just like the old days." He sounded inordinately pleased, and that was confusing. One minute he talked about hating this restaurant as a kid, the next he was delighted to be slicing a tomato "just like the old days." Still, that was *her* tomato he'd just chopped up so efficiently. First he'd commandeered her airplane, and now her tomato.

It seemed ludicrous to be standing here with a man she'd just met, side by side at the kitchen counter, being tutored in the art of slicing tomatoes. But Gwen couldn't keep her gaze from straying toward Robert. He was wearing a shirt of soft herringbone, and she felt an alarming temptation to reach out and finger a sleeve—just to see what the texture of the cloth was like. Gwen stepped around to the other side of the counter before she could succumb.

At the moment Robert was studying her left hand with far too much interest. "That's some rock," he said. "Engagement ring?"

Gwen wiggled the diamond ring on her finger. Even after all this time, she still wasn't used to it. The thing was too darn big. Too big and too modern. Gwen preferred small old-fashioned pieces of jewelry, the sort you might find in someone's attic or half-buried in an antique store. But Scott had been so pleased at surprising her with the ring she hadn't had the heart to tell him how she really felt about it.

"Yes, I'm engaged," she told Robert Beltramo with a touch of defiance.

"So when's the wedding?"

"We haven't set a date yet." This wasn't quite accurate. She'd already postponed the wedding twice, although she couldn't explain exactly why. At twenty-seven, surely she'd had enough experience with men to know which one she should marry. And in every way, Scott Lowell seemed like the perfect choice. She'd promised him that by Christmas Eve she'd finally set a date.

"So, Gwendolyn. How does your future hubby feel about you running a restaurant? It's a hard job—long hours, few vacations. He might not like sharing you with this place."

"Scott understands how I feel about the restaurant. I wouldn't marry someone who didn't understand. And don't call me Gwendolyn."

Robert seemed to enjoy the turn their conversation had taken. "I like the name Gwendolyn. What does this Scott person call you?"

"He calls me Gwen, just like everyone else."

"Are you sure he doesn't call you Gwennie? I like the sound of that, too. Gwendolyn...Gwennie."

She twisted the ring on her finger. "You're not going to get a chance to call me anything, Mr. Beltramo. Because you're going to sell your half of the restaurant to me and then go back to New York City."

"You expect me to leave, and you're not even going to invite me to the wedding?"

Gwen had an urge to hurl her one remaining tomato at him. She wished she could go back to arguing with Robert Beltramo's lawyers, instead of with Robert himself. Already she was far behind on the day's work. She hadn't prepared the pastry filling yet, the chopped vegetables for her eggplant salad still lay uselessly on the counter, her raisin sweet bread definitely looked too crisp, and the Sicilian cake batter was a goner after serving as a runway for her paper airplane. Somehow Gwen had to get control of things.

She tackled the pastry filling, beating ricotta cheese vigorously with sugar and milk. A dollop of the stuff landed on her apron. Robert chuckled. It was a maddening chuckle. She glared at him, which proved to be a mistake. Gwen found herself attracted all over again by the color of his eyes. Amber brown, she decided this time. A color that reminded her of the rich brass and mellow gold of the old-fashioned jewelry she liked. Suddenly her diamond ring seemed more awkward and unwieldy than ever. Another dab of creamy filling landed on her apron.

"Do you plan on leaving anything in the bowl, Gwennie?"

She dumped in a whole bag of chocolate chips. "I'm too busy to wrangle with you anymore, Beltramo. My lawyer will contact your lawyers."

He looked businesslike again, in spite of his rolled-up sleeves and worn jeans. "Forget lawyers. We're going to solve this thing right here, right now. Entertaining as it is to watch you cook, you're out of here, Ferris. Pack your pots. I'm taking over the restaurant."

She dumped candied fruit into her bowl. "Forget it. You're going. I'm the one who's staying."

They stared at each other, and it was obvious they'd reached an impasse. But Gwen refused to back down. No way should Robert Beltramo be allowed to get his hands on this restaurant. He had no appreciation for what she and Pop had built together. He wanted to change things. And he was an all-out exasperating person, apart from everything else. He seemed far too amused at the way she kept twisting her engagement ring on her finger.

"I'm staying," she repeated. "And you, Beltramo, are going!"

CHAPTER TWO

IT WAS VERY EARLY the next morning as Gwen ran along the San Antonio River. She'd hardly been able to sleep last night, disturbed by Robert Beltramo's intrusion into her life. When finally she'd drifted off, she'd dreamed she was arguing with the man all over again. A little after dawn she'd given up hope of peaceful rest. She'd slipped into shorts and a T-shirt and jogged toward the river, hoping to clear her head.

This was a quiet residential section of the River Walk. Gwen took deep breaths of the cool humid air. The lawns of stately Victorian mansions sloped down almost to the water's edge, some of them festively adorned with ceramic Santas and elves. Lush vines curled over arched stone bridges and twined their way up wrought-iron fences. It seemed to Gwen that her thoughts of Robert Beltramo were like those vines, weaving their way tenaciously into her mind. She kept wondering what had happened between Robert and his father. She kept wishing she could understand the man. She told herself that more knowledge about Robert would help her to fight him and win the restaurant. Unfortunately that didn't seem justification enough for all the time she spent ruminating about

him. She was engaged to be married, after all. She
ought to be lost in thoughts of her fiancé!

Gwen ran a little faster, trying to concentrate on
Scott. But in her imagination, sandy-haired, blue-eyed
Scott was quickly superimposed by dark-haired, ha-
zel-eyed Robert Beltramo. She gritted her teeth and
lengthened her stride still farther. Faster, faster, till at
last she'd run him out of her head—

She heard footsteps behind her, then a deep voice.
"Move aside, Ferris. There isn't room enough for the
both of us." A moment later a jogger sailed past her
without even seeming to take a breath—a jogger with
dark wavy hair and broad shoulders.

"What are *you* doing here, Beltramo?" Gwen demanded. "Can't I have peace anywhere?"

"Just taking my morning run," he called back to
her. "I always used to take my run along here. This is
my turf, Gwennie."

"Nobody calls me Gwennie."

"Things change. Things change all the time." And
with that, Robert left her far behind. Gwen pounded
after him, determined to catch up and overtake him.
It took her a few minutes to realize what she was doing. She was falling in with Robert's game, allowing
him to set the pace. Forget that. Gwen slowed delib-
erately to a walk and watched him sprint on ahead.
She had to admit he looked darn good in motion. He
was surely made to run, his body lithe and powerful in
cutoffs and a ragged sweatshirt. And the way he ran
seemed to express an unabashed joy, a sheer exhilaration in movement. Even the air around him seemed
to stir and come joyfully alive....

For crying out loud, she was rhapsodizing about a man out for a jog. Even worse, she was rhapsodizing about Robert Beltramo. Gwen swiveled around and began striding away in the opposite direction. Unfortunately it was only a short while later when she heard footsteps again. His footsteps.

It seemed there was simply no way to get rid of the man! Gwen bent down to tighten her shoelace, waiting for Robert to stroll on by so she could have the path to herself. His legs came into her line of vision and stopped, and she found herself staring at his knees. They were strong, well-formed, masculine knees. Insolent knees. She glared at them.

"Beltramo, this is where I take *my* morning run. Maybe you have some nefarious idea that the more you disrupt my life, the more you can convince me to sell. Forget it."

"I wasn't following you, Gwennie. I live just around the corner from here."

She tied her shoelace too tight and had to start over again. "Are you saying you moved into Pop's old house?"

"Yep. It's my old house, too. I grew up there, remember?"

Gwen stood and began striding down the path. "Damn," she muttered.

Robert matched his pace easily to hers. "What's the problem, Gwennie? Can't understand why you're not happy to see me this morning."

"I wish you'd stop calling me Gwennie. It annoys the heck out of me, in case you hadn't noticed."

"I'd say you got up on the wrong side of the bed today, Gwendolyn." He seemed to relish saying this long-winded version of her name. He gave it a bit of a drawl; even after all his years in New York, he still carried a hint of Texas in his voice.

Gwen stopped and faced him. "It's bad enough you're trying to take over the restaurant. But now you've moved into Pop's house—and that means you and I are practically neighbors."

Robert looked interested. "Neighbors? Where exactly do you live?"

Too late she realized she didn't want to tell him. He'd probably have his lawyers start picketing her house. Or *he'd* start picketing her house. But he'd find out sooner or later where she lived, she was certain of that. No sense in trying to hide it.

"Last year your father told me about a house for sale down the block from him. Something quaintly advertised as 'a handyman's dream.' It needed a lot of work, but it's a very charming Victorian bungalow, and I couldn't pass it up. So I bought it."

"Let me guess. You're talking about the old Sherwood place."

Something in his tone made Gwen uneasy. "Yes, I understand a man named Sherwood built the house in the 1880s."

Robert shook his head. "You're really something, Gwendolyn. That old place is a disaster zone. It was for sale off and on the whole time I was growing up. Nobody could stand the trouble it caused. But now you've come along."

Gwen thought about the leaky pipes, the clogged drains, the haphazard wiring she'd already endured. She didn't appreciate the grin starting on Robert's face.

"I like the house," she said. "Maybe it's a shade rundown, but it has potential. It just needs the right encouragement, that's all."

Now Robert looked thoughtful. "You said the same thing about my father yesterday. You said that underneath all his grouchiness he had potential to be a friendly person—convivial, that's the word you used. And you said he just needed the right encouragement. I think I'm starting to understand you a little better, Gwennie. You go around collecting people and things that everybody else has given up on. That could get to be a pretty cumbersome hobby."

Gwen turned and went down the path again. She hated being analyzed, especially by Robert, but he wouldn't go away. He ambled along beside her, whistling a little under his breath.

"Do you have to be so chipper?" she demanded.

"Can't help myself. You seem to have that effect on me. You make me feel chipper."

She groaned. Usually *she* was a cheerful person. She was used to welcoming each day in a relaxed optimistic manner. But Robert Beltramo put her on edge. Around him, she felt as if she'd been eating nails for breakfast.

Robert looked vibrant from his run, a sheen of sweat on his skin. Damp strands of hair tumbled over his forehead. He gazed ahead as he walked, as if scanning the distance for something no one else could see. Then he looked at Gwen again and smiled.

"Tell me about this fiancé of yours. Is he another lousy-tempered person no one can tolerate but you?"

Gwen gave her engagement ring a twirl. "Of course not. Scott is very outgoing. Everyone likes him. You can't help but like Scott from the first moment you meet him. He came into my restaurant one day for lunch, and it wasn't long before we got engaged. It's great, it really is."

"So what's the problem?"

Gwen frowned. "I didn't say there was any problem. I've just been telling you how...how amiable Scott is."

"Is that what bugs you about him—that he's too amiable? Maybe you prefer the challenge of someone grouchy."

Gwen stopped walking and stared at Robert in exasperation. "Nothing about Scott bugs me. Nothing at all! He's perfect for me. I'm going to marry him very soon, and then the whole thing will be wrapped up."

Another grin was starting on Robert's face. "That's what you call getting married? Wrapping things up?"

"I didn't mean it like that. I'm just trying to say that once I marry Scott, there won't be any more...any more prevaricating."

"So, you've been delaying the wedding. Spit it out, Ferris. Are you saying you don't know whether you should marry the guy or not?"

Gwen wanted to holler, but managed to restrain herself. "Everything about Scott is perfect. Getting engaged to him is the most sensible decision I've ever made."

"But you don't trust sensible decisions, do you?" Robert said in a wise tone. "You'd rather buy a decrepit house nobody else wants, or hang around an ornery old man who alienated half the population of Texas when he was alive."

Gwen tugged on her engagement ring so hard that it popped right off her finger. It arced through the air, flashing in the sunlight, and plunked down in a tangled patch of winter grass. She stood frozen for a moment, but then she hurried off the path and began scrabbling for it. Robert knelt beside her.

"Take it easy. We'll find it. A rock that big won't disappear."

"Well, it seems to have. I can't find it anywhere." Gwen patted the grass. She dug through it. But the engagement ring had vanished as if it had never existed.

"Hold on," Robert said. "You're doing this all wrong. You're plowing through here like a tractor run amok. You have to be organized about it."

"I just lost a diamond the size of King Kong's nose, and you're telling me to be organized?"

"That's exactly what I'm telling you." Robert bent his head close to the ground and started probing the area methodically, inch by inch. Well, easy for *him* to be calm. He wasn't the one who'd lost the darn thing. Gwen sat back with a thump. Of course, she knew how Scott would react to something like this. He wouldn't be angry. He'd be concerned, he'd be sympathetic. He'd be understanding.

Gwen watched Robert proceed with his methodical search. "How would you react if this was your ring?" she asked. "I mean, supposing you had a fiancée and she lost the ring you had given her, what would you do?"

Robert straightened up a little. He rubbed his jaw, appearing to give the matter a great deal of thought. Then he nodded. "I'd tell her that subconsciously she'd lost the ring on purpose. I'd tell her it indicated severe prevarication on her part. I'd tell her she wasn't sure whether or not she wanted to marry me."

Gwen frowned. "I didn't lose the ring on purpose. It was an accident."

"I thought we were talking a hypothetical situation here," Robert pointed out. "My fiancée. My ring."

"Yes, of course. That's what we're talking about." Gwen poked her fingers through the grass. Robert went back to his search, his nose close to the ground. From here Gwen had a good view of his wavy hair. Dynamic hair, that's what he had, the kind that wouldn't kowtow to any comb. Scott's hair, on the other hand, was lanky and straight and cut a trifle too short. Gwen hadn't realized it until precisely this moment, but Scott's hair was unimaginative. No other word for it.

Gwen felt disloyal. "You know, Scott doesn't have a suspicious mind like you, Beltramo. He'd never accuse me of losing his ring on purpose. He'd pat me on the back and try to comfort me, and then he'd just call his insurance company and report the ring missing."

"Right."

"That *is* right. He's a good man, and I'm very lucky."

"Keep trying to convince yourself, Gwendolyn. Sooner or later it's bound to work."

Gwen fell silent. She was engaged to Scott Lowell, and he was a wonderful man. The best. Somehow she'd figure out why she'd been unable to set a wedding date. Yes, she'd figure it out. By Christmas Eve she'd have the matter resolved.

For the moment, Gwen sat cross-legged in the grass and listened to the murmuring calls of pigeons. She gazed at the dark mysterious water of the river and began to enjoy her surroundings. She'd always been enchanted with the river. The city had grown up along these banks, and the river was still the center, the heart of San Antonio. It was in Gwen's heart, too. One of the reasons she'd applied for work at Pop's Restaurant all those years ago was the building's location right on the River Walk—the exotic Paseo del Rio.

Gwen leaned back, lifting her face to the gentle December sunlight. It took her a few minutes to feel guilty because she'd stopped searching for the ring. She was allowing Robert to do all the work. But her left hand felt so...free. So unencumbered. She wanted to enjoy that sensation a little while longer.

"Aha," Robert said, holding up the ring. "Found the bruiser. I told you all it would involve was an organized effort."

The ring sparkled in the sun. Gwen stared at it, not making any move to take it from Robert. At last he was the one who stirred.

"Give me your hand."

With an odd reluctance, Gwen held out her left hand. Robert took hold of it and slipped the ring onto her finger. His touch was warm, as warm as the sunlight. He didn't release her hand right away. Instead, he gazed down at it, his eyebrows drawn together quizzically. Gwen caught her breath a little. It was absurd, having Robert Beltramo slip another man's engagement ring onto her finger. And yet his touch felt so right....

Gwen snatched her hand away. "Thank you for finding the ring," she said in a constrained voice.

"You're welcome." The amusement was back in his face, glimmering in his amber-brown eyes.

"I've figured it out," she said. "Why I've been delaying the wedding. I've gotten used to being on my own, that's all. Marriage is a big change. It's enough to make anybody hesitate a little."

"Hmm. That's an adequate theory. But—"

"It's more than a theory. Listen, I've dated a lot of men who were downright jerks. And then I met Scott, someone genuinely decent. Men like that don't come along very often. I'd be a real fool to turn him down just because I've been single a long time, and I'm comfortable being single."

"I'm not arguing with you, Gwennie. You're arguing with yourself."

Gwen scrambled to her feet, unable to sit still any longer. Robert Beltramo had a way of making her feel as if she had ants crawling up her socks. Her brief enjoyment of the morning had evaporated, and all of a sudden the sun was too hot. As she pulled a handkerchief out of her pocket to wipe the perspiration from her face, several slips of paper fluttered to the ground like confetti. That was all she needed! More bits and pieces of her life exposed to Robert. He picked up the scraps of paper, then stood to hold them out to her. His expression was solemn, but she could tell he was still amused by her. She'd already overexplained about Scott, and now she began overexplaining again.

"Those must be recipes," she said. "I'm always jotting down recipes. The other day I came across a great one for ravioli..." Goodness, why couldn't she clam up? All her life she'd been a listener, not a talker. She liked it that way. But around Robert all sorts of embarrassing revelations seemed to rattle out of her mouth.

He glanced down at one of the slips of paper and read out loud. " 'Doze in the garden all morning with your favorite book in your lap. Go fishing all afternoon...' This is a recipe?"

She snatched the scraps of paper from him and stuffed them back into her pocket. "That happens to be Mrs. Alexander's recipe for a perfect day. She's a customer of mine, a wonderful woman of eighty-five. She comes in every night for dinner."

"And you write down her memoirs on shreds of paper?"

"Whatever's handy. Mrs. Alexander likes it when I write down what she says. Makes her feel she'll be preserved on paper, at least. After your father died, she got scared she'd be next. I try to reassure her that everything's going to be okay." Gwen didn't mention that once she'd outlined Mrs. Alexander's extensive genealogy on the back of a menu. She doubted Robert would understand; he'd probably just see it as a waste of a menu.

"Are you that sociable with all your customers?" he asked. Talking about the restaurant, he was starting to sound businesslike, almost brusque. Gwen felt defensive. She hated feeling that way, but being around Robert made her want to build walls against him—walls as thick and strong as the Alamo.

"My customers talk to me about a lot of different things. I think of them as a sort of family. It's like having aunts and uncles and cousins...."

"Sounds like you collect oddball customers, along with everything else. And you treat them like long-lost relatives."

"Nothing's wrong with my customers." Gwen blotted her face, and now Robert gave her elegant lace handkerchief a skeptical glance. She knew ordinary tissues were more practical, but she couldn't resist the old-fashioned ones—even if they weren't exactly the accessory you'd expect with cotton shorts and a T-shirt. She stuffed the elegant lace back into her pocket. She'd had enough of Robert's looking her over and analyzing her as if she were some kind of noodle-head. This morning she'd already given him far too much ammunition against her. She'd betrayed those vague niggling doubts about her engagement, that was the worst of it. But it was time to go on the offensive, instead of standing by as Robert took potshots at her life.

"Beltramo, I know you want to take over the restaurant, but I won't let you do it. It's going to stay my place, and I'll collect any kind of customers I please. You can darn well go back to New York."

"You're a stubborn woman, Gwennie."

"Yes. I am." She stood squarely on the river path as Robert studied her. After a moment he shook his head.

"I thought for sure Plan A would work. Put a lot of effort into it," he grumbled. "Had my lawyers offer you a generous price, came out here myself to negotiate, but you still won't budge."

"You've got that much right."

He gazed into the distance once more, obviously mulling over the situation. "Okay, Plan A didn't work. Time to try Plan B."

Gwen shifted her weight uneasily. "What are you talking about?"

"I'm still working out the details. But it's good. Plan B is damn good." He looked intense—and suddenly quite happy, of all things. Gwen had a foreboding that this new idea of his wouldn't make *her* happy.

"Don't try building the suspense," she said. "Just tell me. What on earth is Plan B?"

He smiled. "It's simple. You won't sell your half of the restaurant, so you and I are going to work together."

"Oh, no!"

"For a limited amount of time. A week, say. I predict that after one week of sharing the restaurant with me, you'll be begging to sell. You'll be so grateful to get out you won't know what to do." Robert flexed a little, as if getting ready to sweep Gwen aside and barrel down the path. She knew her first impression of him was a hundred percent correct: he was a man who needed action, who craved motion. She suspected he thrived on it, no matter who or what got in his way.

And now *she* was in his way. Well, she'd have to stay there. Gwen straddled the path, her feet planted firmly. "I don't like Plan B. Forget Plan B. Nix Plan B."

"What choice do you have, Gwennie? We each own fifty percent. We're partners, like it or not. And all it will take is one week. By next Saturday night, no later than 10:00 p.m. central time, you'll be willing to sign those papers my lawyers keep waving under your nose."

"You think you'll drive me crazy, Beltramo? It that it?"

"No question. I'm already driving you crazy. It won't take much more to do you in."

Damn, he was really enjoying himself now. His expressive face showed it. Gwen was beginning to realize something else about Robert Beltramo. He liked having obstacles—and overcoming them.

Somehow she had to be an obstacle that couldn't be overcome. But he was right about one thing. The two of them were fifty-fifty partners. At the moment they both had equal claim on the restaurant. Gwen had to make that work to her advantage. She had no other choice.

"All right," she said slowly. "You're on. We'll run the restaurant together for one week. But I'm wagering that by Saturday night—10:00 p.m. central time— you'll be the one begging to sell. Because you won't be able to tolerate working in that place very long. You hated it as a kid, and you couldn't wait to get away. Maybe you have some nostalgic idea about coming back at Christmastime, but you'll want to get away again. You don't belong there.''

His features tightened, but only for a moment. "It's a wager, then—one that I'm going to win. Let's shake on it." He took her hand in a firm grasp, and again she was unsettled by his touch. They stared into each other's eyes. Gwen cursed herself for being the first to glance away. Robert let go of her hand, and she folded her arms against her body. A squirrel darted across the grass and sprang up a tree. The pigeons murmured under the bridge, and the dark river flowed by.

Gwen continued to block the path, but Robert merely dodged around her and went running off along the riverbank.

"See you later, Gwennie," he called back, and she swore she heard laughter in his voice. Gwen swiveled and stared after him. It was going to be one heck of a week battling Robert Beltramo, but in the end she'd win.

She had to win.

CHAPTER THREE

A SHORT WHILE LATER, Gwen turned her key in the door of the restaurant and strode inside. The place was deserted. This early in the morning her two employees hadn't yet arrived for work, and Robert hadn't arrived, either. Good. For a little while Gwen could have the restaurant to herself. For a few moments, at least, she could harbor the illusion that nothing had changed here, that Robert Beltramo hadn't come barreling into her life.

She hurried through the dining area and into the kitchen. The glass star hanging at the window sent beams of amethyst and sapphire light into the room. The wooden countertops shone the color of rich honey, and burnished copper pots hung suspended from a butcher's rail like a cluster of upside-down flowers. A bouquet of paper poinsettias on one of the counters added another splash of color. Gwen loved working in this kitchen. She loved the brightness of it, and the clutter she herself had created on the shelves: rolling pins and ravioli cutters and pizza pans, cake molds in every shape and size, narrow cruets of shining aquamarine, earthenware crocks and cheese dishes and pudding bowls. Everything was piled in a jum-

ble, a delightful disorder that was essential for creative cooking.

Gwen pulled some spinach from the fridge to make
lasagna noodles and poured cornmeal into a sauce-
pan for her famous polenta. But right away something was wrong; she couldn't work with her usual
concentration. It was her own fault. Instead of wearing her old jeans and one of her polo shirts, this
morning she'd changed into an elegant silk dress. She
knew she looked good in this dress; the slim waistline
showed off her figure, and the dark jade color complemented her blue-gray eyes. But she couldn't push
up the long narrow sleeves to get them out of her way.
And of course she couldn't put on an apron, because
that would ruin the effect of her outfit.

Gwen was disgusted with herself. She hadn't wanted
to admit it before, but she knew why she'd rigged herself up like this. She'd wanted to look good for Robert Beltramo, of all people. She'd wanted to impress
the very man who threatened to take over Pop's Restaurant.

What had gotten into her? She was supposed to go
to this kind of trouble for her fiancé, not for anyone
else. Gwen wiggled her fingers in frustration, holding
her hands out awkwardly from her body so she
wouldn't get cornmeal on her dress. Robert Beltramo
chose this moment to stroll into the kitchen. He
looked fresh and energetic after his morning run, his
hair still damp from the shower. He wore canvas
trousers and a white cotton shirt that reminded Gwen
of wash fluttering on a clothesline on a sunny Texas
morning. His casual clothes immediately made her feel

absurdly overdressed. She wiggled her fingers again, frustration mounting, her arms still jutted out awkwardly. Robert leaned against the doorjamb and surveyed her.

"Let me guess. You're in the middle of performing some strange medieval rite. No—you're trying to put a curse on me. That's it—you're putting a hex on me so I'll go back to New York and leave the restaurant to you. No chance, Ferris. No chance."

Her face burning, Gwen rinsed her hands at the sink. Then she grabbed one of her big aprons and wrapped it around her body. She tied the strings in an extra-strong knot. "I'm just trying to get some work done, that's all." She started snapping stalks off spinach leaves, and Robert went on watching her. She wished she hadn't worn her best antique earrings today, the ones shaped like small roses in swirls of gold and delicate pink enamel. She'd even pinned her hair up in loose curls so the earrings would show off better. With her luck, Robert would guess she'd done all this solely for his benefit. And he'd be amused by it, sure as anything. Look at that smile already lurking on his face.

Gwen ripped a spinach leaf in two. She didn't understand herself at all. She found Robert annoying, irritating and just plain provoking. Yet when he looked at her, she wanted to see a spark of admiration in his eyes—not the laughter glimmering there now.

He came to stand across the counter from her, and fiddled with her pastry brush. Gwen snatched it away, but that didn't stop him. He started poking his nose into her cupboards. "What did you do here, set off a bomb? This is an explosion of dishes and pans."

"I know where everything is. I have things arranged exactly the way I like them." Gwen sprinkled some water into her cornmeal. "Listen, Robert. Let's set some ground rules about this week. Number one, I'll remain the head chef. Number two—"

"No rules, Gwennie. What's the point of having a wager if we set up rules? The whole idea is to drive the other person bonkers to the point of capitulation. Isn't that what we agreed?"

He was already driving her bonkers. He began foraging through her ladles and spatulas and mallets. It seemed Robert felt compelled to examine everything—and with a critical air.

Gwen rattled her pan of cornmeal on the stove. "Here's the bottom line. There's room for only one of us in this kitchen. I have a lot of work to do, so why don't you just leave me to it?"

He took one of Gwen's dish towels and tucked it into the waist of his trousers. The towel was decorated with a vivid pattern of Christmas trees and somehow it only made Robert look more debonair. He picked up a ladle and brandished it about. "Move over, Gwennie. I'm going to show you some real cooking."

Oh, no. This was going to be even worse than Gwen had thought. She hadn't actually expected the man to *cook*. He was an advertising executive who needed action, motion, in his life. Surely he'd be able to take only so much of slicing tomatoes and such. But here he was, waving a ladle like someone warming up to conduct a symphony orchestra.

"Okay," he said, "where's the lunch menu?"

"You don't need to see it. Go poke around in the dining room, why don't you?"

He rolled up his sleeves. "Move over, Gwennie. And give me the menu."

Gwen considered trying to throw him out of the kitchen physically, but instead, she slapped a tattered piece of paper down. He picked it up and dangled it as if it were an overcooked noodle.

"Does everything you touch get spots on it?" he asked. "This thing is covered with coffee stains, dried jam and who knows what else. I don't see how anybody could read it."

"I don't have to read it. I know each day's menu by heart."

He held the sheet of paper up to his nose as if that would help him decipher it. "Hmm. Amaretti, linguine, cannoli, rigatoni..."

Gwen stirred her cornmeal a bit too vigorously. The way Robert savored those words on his tongue, she could almost see visions of Italy shimmering in front of her: the Bay of Naples, Lake Como, the islands of Capri. She'd never been to Italy, but just listening to Robert's rich pronunciation made all the travel posters she'd ever seen come to life. His voice awakened in her the secret yearning she'd always had to visit certain places—Milan and Rome, Florence and Verona.

"...timballo, pastiera, maccheroni..." Robert seemed more and more caught up in the words himself, as if rediscovering a language that had been lost to him. Gwen wished he would stop. She didn't want any uncomfortable yearnings stirred inside her. She didn't have any *place* for such inconvenient longings. After all, Scott had never made her dream of Italy...

Gwen clapped a lid over her polenta. Maybe she'd get to Italy someday, maybe not. Either way, it wouldn't have anything to do with Robert Beltramo.

"All right, you've read the menu," she said. "You can cross that off your list."

"I'm just getting started. First thing I'm going to do is make the tortoni."

"That happens to be one of my specialties," Gwen protested.

"You'll probably tell me that everything on this menu is your specialty."

"Well, as a matter of fact..."

"I make damn good tortoni." The glint in Robert's eyes was ominous. He was like a man on a mission. Gwen decided her wisest course for the moment was to step aside and let him go at it. Maybe his urge for cooking wouldn't last very long.

She watched as he gathered his ingredients—whipping cream, almonds, macaroons, vanilla. He did everything with a brisk economy of motion, no wasted gestures, each action leading to a specific goal. Basically, he didn't putter—unlike Gwen, who liked to putter around the kitchen whenever time permitted. She would gaze at the river and breathe in the pungent aroma of herbs drying on the windowsill. She'd rummage through shelves of food simply for the pleasure of it. Even on the busiest days she knew how to take a pause now and then to replenish her spirit.

But it was obvious Robert hadn't yet learned the art of relaxed cooking. He made his tortoni with all the intensity and concentration of a train engineer determined to run on schedule.

Gwen looked on as Robert chopped almonds, crushed macaroons and whipped cream without creating any mess—not one spatter on the counter, not one splat on his shirt. "I don't trust a clean cook," she said with disdain. "I never have. Shows you're not involved with your food."

"You can be a decent chef without looking like you've just had a collision with a pineapple torte. Remember that, Ferris." The glint in Robert's eyes was growing more dangerous all the time; he seemed to enjoy cooking. The next thing she knew, he'd want to whip up some anchovy dip or even make some eggplant parmigiana. Before things got completely out of hand, she had to distract him. It seemed only appropriate to remind him about the world he'd left behind in New York.

"You know, your lawyers told me you run a successful advertising agency. They told me about that commercial you made for television—the one where three guys who look just like the Marx Brothers fight over the last jar of spaghetti sauce. I've seen it a couple of times on TV myself. It's funny and charming, and your lawyers said it even won awards."

Robert was rapidly spooning his whipped-cream mixture into dessert dishes. "I didn't know my lawyers were so damn talkative."

"When you consider all the letters they've written to me and all the visits they've made here, after a while they did get talkative. It was only natural."

"I don't suppose you encouraged them any," he remarked dryly.

"I like to hear what people have to say. And after learning about this big advertising agency of yours, I don't understand how you could just walk away from it."

Robert ferried a tray of dessert dishes over to the freezer. "I'm keeping tabs on things in New York. And my partners are very competent people. They can handle things while I'm away."

"It sounds like you don't actually plan to stay in San Antonio. This is more like a holiday leave for you, isn't it?"

"Don't get too hopeful, Ferris. I'm keeping my share of the advertising agency, but that doesn't mean I won't be spending all the time I want in San Antonio running this restaurant." He stared into the freezer after he'd finished finding room for his desserts. "What do you do—use this thing for target practice? Looks like you fling stuff in here from the other side of the kitchen."

Gwen went to push the freezer door shut. "I have my own kind of order. But I just don't understand it— advertising has to be something tremendously exciting. How can you decide to spend your time here, away from all that action?"

He roved the kitchen, apparently looking for his next project. "After selling a million jars of spaghetti sauce, maybe I need something different in my life."

"And you think making spaghetti sauce, instead of selling it, is the answer?"

"Damn right it is. This restaurant is a challenge, Gwennie. That's what I need in my life right now, a new challenge. By the way, that pan on the grill is about to self-destruct."

Darn! She'd forgotten all about her polenta. She snatched the pan from the heat, but it was too late. The cornmeal was scorched. She stared at it in mortification. Usually she could juggle ten different things in the kitchen at once. But today... today Robert Beltramo was here.

He took down a pan hanging from the butcher-block railing. A few moments later the sizzle of butter came from the grill, and then the ping-ping-ping of rice landing in the simmering butter. Gwen frowned. Robert was making cooking sounds that were altogether too pleasant. He was even whistling under his breath. Unfortunately Gwen liked the sound of a whistled tune. Scott couldn't whistle to save his life....

Gwen curled the fingers of her left hand and felt the diamond on her engagement ring dig into her palm. Lately she'd taken to wearing the ring so the diamond was on the inside of her finger—where she wouldn't always have to look at that big showy rock. But the diamond was making its presence well known right this minute, its sharp edges jabbing her flesh.

Gwen's two employees arrived, and Robert succeeded in irritating her all over again—announcing peremptorily that he was calling a staff meeting in the dining area to begin in exactly three minutes.

Gwen cornered him. "Hold on, Beltramo. This isn't how I operate around here. I never call staff meetings. If something needs to be discussed, we talk it out over coffee and pastry."

"I get it. Kind of like a family chat."

"Exactly. And it works very well. Both Claudine and Jeremy know they can talk to me about whatever's bothering them, any time of the day. I'm always ready to listen."

"Ferris, staff meetings are so you can tell employees what *you* want, not the other way around. Maybe you ought to take a course in management." Robert gave her a smile that could only be termed condescending.

"Sounds like you've had one management course too many," Gwen retorted. "Victorian literature, that's what I studied. Read Charles Dickens, and maybe you'll learn a little something about human nature."

Robert had turned solemn, but his mouth gave a suspicious twitch. "Dickens, huh? Next you'll be telling me *The Pickwick Papers* is actually a manual on how to run a restaurant."

"Now that you mention it, *The Pickwick Papers* is exactly what you need. I recommend you spend some time with Captain Boldwig and Mr. Raddle and Dr. Slammer. It'll do you all sorts of good. And you won't have time for any ridiculous staff meetings."

"In case you've forgotten, Gwennie, you and I are partners. Your employees are my employees. And I happen to like staff meetings. Get a big kick out of 'em."

Gwen blocked the door to the dining room and tried to stare Robert down. It was useless, of course. She couldn't get around the fact that she and Robert were fifty-fifty partners. If he wanted a darn staff meeting, he had every right to hold one. After a moment Gwen stepped aside.

"Go to it. Give us all a lesson in managerial expertise."

Robert ignored the mockery in her voice. He ushered her into the dining room, pulling out a chair for her beside Jeremy and Claudine as if she were simply another employee. But she refused to be relegated to a secondary position. She remained standing.

"Jeremy, Claudine," she said, "this is Mr. Robert Beltramo, Pop's son. I don't want you to be disturbed by his presence in any way. You can go about your work as usual. He'll only be here a short while— a *very* short while."

Robert gave her one of his sardonic glances, then strode to the head of the table. "What Ms. Ferris is trying to tell you is that she and I are partners now. That makes me your employer, too. You'll find that I'm very fair, as long as you're both willing to work hard. Because that's what I expect to see around here—hard work." Robert paused, standing there like a feudal lord surveying his vassals. He stared at Gwen as if the very force of his gaze would compel her to sit down. The man was high-handed, domineering and arrogant, to boot!

Gwen stewed for a moment, but finally she had no other choice than to sit. She scooted her chair close to the table and rearranged the centerpiece—a small basket filled with Christmas-tree ornaments and topped with a red bow. She waited for Robert to continue, impatient to have the wretched meeting over with as soon as possible.

"This restaurant is headed for some exciting changes," he said. "Business is going to grow at a fast rate. Eventually we'll expand the operation. Things won't be stagnating the way they are right now."

Gwen's resolution to be calm promptly disintegrated. "This place isn't stagnating!" she protested. "And we already have as much business as we can handle. People come here precisely because they want a relaxed atmosphere."

Robert didn't appear to be listening to her. He focused his attention on Jeremy and Claudine.

"New advancement opportunities will be opening up," he told them. "If you put in the right amount of effort, you can both be part of the changes ahead."

He was talking to the wrong crowd. Jeremy looked downright uncooperative. Jeremy, of course, always looked uncooperative; that was a natural part of his demeanor. He slouched in his chair with a bored expression on his face. Twenty years old, Jeremy had worked at Pop's Restaurant for the past ten months as a combination dishwasher/busboy. Usually he spoke in monosyllables, when he spoke at all. He was a good worker but manifested absolutely no ambition. It was clear Robert wouldn't inspire Jeremy with offers of advancement.

Claudine, on the other hand, seemed inspired by Robert's attractiveness. She was gazing at him with a dreamy expression, as if she didn't care what he said just as long as he went on speaking. Claudine was a pretty red-haired waitress who had been at the restaurant almost two years. An aspiring dancer, she often wore leotards with her uniform, as if to prove to the world that she wasn't really a waitress. Now Claudine sat with a graceful posture that seemed a bit too studied, obviously for Robert's benefit. Well, she could be forgiven a little feminine interest in the man. Unfortunately Robert was as handsome as he was arrogant.

Robert paced back and forth in front of the table. "All right, I can see what needs to be done here," he muttered. "Somebody needs to get the blood pumping with this crew. And I know just the way to do it." Robert glanced around the restaurant for a moment with a slight frown. Then he spied the chalkboard that Gwen used to announce the daily specials. He hauled the chalkboard over beside the table, stand and all. Without ceremony he erased Gwen's proclamation of "Free Strawberries with Every Sausage Pie." He began drawing a diagram on the board with bold strokes of chalk. A large rectangle with a line slashed down the middle, some lopsided circles, an X jotted here and there...

"If you're trying to play ticktacktoe, you have a lot to learn," Gwen observed.

"This happens to be a basketball court." He gestured rather proudly at his diagram. "Gwendolyn, you're going to play basketball. We're all going to play basketball. I'm forming a team here."

Jeremy actually perked up a little, sitting straighter in his chair. Claudine looked alert, too, smoothing the knees of her turquoise leotards. But Gwen only laughed.

"You have to be joking, Beltramo. A basketball team? Where'd you get a cockeyed idea like that?"

"Somebody's got to stir up this apathetic crowd, Ferris. Can't think of a better way to do it. Besides, I hear the parking valets at the Roosevelt Hotel already have a team in action. And we'll have to work damn hard to get ourselves in shape if we're going to challenge them."

"Challenge them—why in blazes would you want to do that?"

He raised his eyebrows slightly. "Ferris, it ought to be self-evident. People work better together when they share the camaraderie of team sports. It's a sound management technique implemented by many companies. Besides, I finally have a chance to make a team work. My partners at the advertising agency were just too out of shape. This'll be different. The three of you definitely have something for me to work with."

Robert sounded full of enthusiasm, and he sounded determined, too. Gwen had an ominous feeling about this. She was already beginning to suspect that Robert allowed few obstacles to stand in his way. She imagined the scenario he'd left behind in New York: several portly advertising executives spread out flat on a basketball court, their sneakers pointing in the air because they hadn't been able to keep up with Robert.

Now he jabbed his piece of chalk toward the blackboard. "Okay, the sooner you get familiar with your positions, the better. Jeremy will play point guard.

Claudine will be a forward. As for you, Ferris, you'll be the other forward. I'll play center. That still leaves us one player short. How about your fiancé, Gwendolyn?''

"Forget it." Gwen scowled at Robert. "As far as I know, Scott's never even touched a basketball."

"Figures. But it doesn't really matter. We can challenge the other team's best four, if it comes down to that." Robert jotted some more *X*s on the blackboard in a purposeful manner. There was no longer any doubt about it. Robert Beltramo was on the move again with a new plan, a new goal.

Gwen wadded up a napkin, thoroughly rankled. "Robert, maybe you've noticed that not a single one of us has agreed to your crazy plan. And this restaurant happens to be a democracy."

"No problem. I'll take a vote." Robert pointed his piece of chalk straight at Jeremy. "You'll be on the team."

It sounded more like a mandate than a vote. But Jeremy didn't seem to mind. He gave what appeared to be a nod of agreement before slouching in his chair again.

Claudine spoke up. "Mr. Beltramo, I'm a dancer, not a basketball player. I have my career to think about. Rehearsals, auditions—you know how it is. I don't have time for much else."

Robert pointed his chalk at her. "You join my team, and I promise you'll see the benefits in your career right away. Increased stamina, higher jumps—you'll be dancing like never before."

Claudine jiggled one of her legs, as if she could already see herself bounding to new heights. But she still seemed hesitant. "Well, I don't know..."

"Sure, you do." Robert's piece of chalk stabbed the air again. "Here's the story. There's a hoop out back of the restaurant—I put it up myself a long time ago. We'll meet there at three o'clock today for our first practice session. I'll expect every one of you. Meeting dismissed."

Jeremy slouched out of the room. Claudine still hadn't committed herself to the idea, although she seemed determined to demonstrate her muscle tone for Robert. Rising from her chair, she drifted gracefully past him. She seemed on the verge of executing a pirouette, but finally disappeared into the kitchen.

Robert stood for a moment, surveying his diagram with far too much satisfaction. Give the man a piece of chalk, and he was even more dangerous than he was brandishing a ladle. Gwen could no longer control herself. She marched up to him, seized the chalk and scrawled in big letters across his diagram: "OUT TO LUNCH."

"Gwennie, I can tell you don't have the proper team spirit. You'll have to do something about that, and fast. Our first game with the Roosevelt Rough Riders is coming right up."

She barely stifled a moan. "Let me guess. Your team is going to be called the Beltramo Buccaneers."

Robert looked thoughtful. "Hey, I like the sound of that."

This was getting worse and worse. She gazed at him in exasperation. "Listen, I'm not going to be on your blasted team. That would be like . . . like . . ."

"Like going over to the enemy?" he suggested. He smiled at her, and right then she realized they were standing much too close. After this morning in the kitchen, an enticing aroma of basil and oregano emanated from him. She backed away and almost knocked over the chalkboard.

"For one thing, I don't know how to play basketball," she declared. "And second—"

"I'm a good coach, Gwennie. After I'm through with you, you'll love the game." He was grinning now.

"Forget it," she muttered, gripping the chalk.

"What are you afraid of?" he asked. "That you might actually have some fun?"

Oh, yes, she was afraid of that—afraid that if she didn't watch herself, she *would* have too much fun around Robert Beltramo. He was too full of life and vibrancy. If she allowed herself to go chasing up and down a basketball court with him, what next? Whatever happened, she didn't want to be disloyal to Scott. She wouldn't tolerate that; loyalty was too important to her.

Gwen crammed the piece of chalk into her apron pocket. "I won't be on your team. I can't stop Jeremy and Claudine, if they decide it's what they want, but count me out." She began striding toward the kitchen, only to have Robert's voice follow her.

"We're already playing ball, Gwennie—you and me. You can't escape that."

She turned and stared at him. "Watch out for me, Beltramo. Because I'm on the offensive here, not the defensive."

His grin widened. "That's what I like to hear. Something tells me you'd make a fine basketball player. I'll get you out on that court yet."

"Not a chance, Beltramo. Not a chance!"

CHAPTER FOUR

GWEN STIFLED a weary yawn as she tossed some carrots and lettuce into a paper bag. The overhead lights in the kitchen shone down softly, deepening the red of the chili-pepper wreaths on the wall and glinting off the cluster of silver bells that adorned one corner. It was late evening, and the last of the dinner crowd was finally out the door, the last pot finally scoured clean. Jeremy and Claudine had already gone home, and Robert had disappeared. Gwen could only hope he'd gone home, too. She needed a few minutes to herself. She needed to reclaim her restaurant after this first exasperating day with Robert Beltramo. If one day could unsettle her so much, how on earth would she make it until next Saturday night?

She *had* to make it, that was all. She had to do it for Pop's sake, and for her own sake, too. She couldn't allow Robert to change this delightful homey place into some fast-paced business venture.

"Absconding with the vegetables, Gwennie?"

She jumped at the sound of Robert's voice behind her, and almost sent a carrot flying through the air. "Darn, I thought you'd left."

"Still here. I know how much you enjoy my company." He leaned against the doorjamb, hands stuffed in the pockets of his canvas trousers. Somehow he still looked vibrant and energetic after his day of jostling Gwen in the kitchen. But it had been a successful day for him in many ways. He'd found no difficulty in prodding Jeremy out to the basketball hoop—and it had taken only a little persuasion to get Claudine out there dribbling a ball, too. Just like that, Robert had commandeered both Gwen's employees. He hadn't even acted perturbed when Gwen adamantly refused to join the game; the man seemed to possess unbounded confidence that eventually he'd get his own way.

He'd also made an impression as a chef. Some of Gwen's pickiest dinner customers had enthused about Robert's linguine-and-clam-sauce, and one entire table had asked for seconds of his tortoni. Gwen had sampled the tortoni herself, annoyed to find it delicious, the chilled cream smooth and sweet in her mouth.

Now Gwen tossed one more head of lettuce into her paper sack. "If you must know, these vegetables are no longer fresh enough to use. Instead of throwing them out, I'm taking them home to Whiskers. And before you make any cracks, let me inform you that Whiskers is my rabbit."

Robert managed to remain solemn. "Hey, I'd never make jokes about anything named Whiskers. Sounds like my kind of rabbit."

"He's not a sociable creature. All he wants right now is to munch his carrots in peace." Gwen untied her apron and hung it on a peg. She took her sack of vegetables and, striding to the kitchen door, tried to maneuver past Robert. He deftly took the bag from her.

"Come on," he said. "I'll walk you home."

"You don't have to do that. Really."

"Is your boyfriend coming to pick you up?"

Gwen turned the ring on her finger. "Scott's out of town on business."

"Wondered why I hadn't seen him around."

"Scott travels a lot for his job selling computer software. And he just got a promotion. That means he's been traveling even more the past few weeks. He works hard, you know."

Robert nodded gravely. "I see."

Gwen thought she heard something suspicious in his tone. "Beltramo, exactly what is it you see?"

"Nothing but what you told me, Ferris. You're marrying some hardworking guy who's off selling computer programs, instead of mooning around his fiancée." Robert started walking through the dining area with the sack of vegetables. Gwen switched off the lights and hurried after him. In the darkness she bumped into him, automatically placing one hand against his back to steady herself. She could feel his warmth through the soft cotton of his shirt, and she quickly removed her hand.

"I certainly don't want someone who gets all moony around me," she told Robert as they went outside. "I mean, there's nothing sappy about Scott, thank goodness. He's very steady, very dependable. That's what I need."

"Sure, Gwennie. A guy has to get ahead. If it means spending less time with his girl, that's the way it is."

Robert sounded completely serious, but Gwen still didn't trust him. She walked along the river at his side, watching the holiday lights cast a glimmer on the mysterious water. Usually Gwen was soothed when she gazed into the river, but tonight uncomfortable longings stirred inside her.

"You've probably been in the same situation yourself," Gwen said. "You've probably found yourself working hard, not able to spend much time with your girlfriend."

Now Robert seemed thoughtful. He took a moment to answer. "Most of the women I've dated have been busy with their own careers. I guess I haven't met anyone yet who could induce me to spend less time at work. I can imagine it happening, though." The teasing note crept back into his voice. "I can imagine some lady sweeping me off my feet and making me forget about everything else in my life."

"Right." Gwen briskly climbed the steps of a stone bridge arching over the water. She was about to go on, but Robert stopped in the middle of the bridge and balanced the sack of carrots and lettuce on the balustrade.

"You don't believe me, Ferris? It's the truth. If the right girl ever comes along, I'll do all sorts of crazy things for her. I'll forget to show up for work entirely, and next thing you know I'll take her off to Mexico or Alaska."

Gwen tried to think of a flippant retort, but her brain wouldn't cooperate. A poignant Spanish ballad floated through the air; somewhere down the river mariachi players were singing and strumming their guitars.

"Mexico," Gwen murmured, studying Robert's profile in the starlight. "Mexico would be fine, I suppose. But I've always wanted to go to Italy, myself." Instantly she wished she hadn't let the words slip out. Her dreams of Italy were secret, meant only for herself. Robert turned toward her, but she couldn't read his expression in the darkness.

"Is that where you'll go on your honeymoon, Gwen? L'Italia?"

A shiver ran through her, a shiver she blamed on the cool night air. She didn't want to be affected by Robert's nearness or by the sensual exotic sound of his voice. Yet still, she lingered beside him on the bridge.

"Scott and I won't be able to take a long honeymoon. We'll probably spend a weekend in Galveston, and then—"

"I know. Then he'll have to get right back to selling those computer programs."

"You're one to talk," Gwen said defensively. "You joke about being reckless if the 'right girl' comes along, but I don't believe it for a second. You'll just go barreling through life, and you won't stop to be romantic. I'm already starting to know you, Beltramo."

He gave a low soft laugh that seemed to blend with the mellow Spanish music. "Don't count on it, Gwennie. For all you know, I may be full of surprises. I may be the most romantic guy around."

"I don't believe *any* man is truly romantic." Gwen went down the steps on the other side of the bridge, her heels clicking on the stone. She walked fast, but Robert barely had to quicken his pace to stay beside her. He balanced the sack in the crook of one arm.

"It's all becoming clear," he said. "You settled for this Scott fellow because you've given up on romance. That explains everything."

Gwen brought herself up short and glared at Robert. "I didn't *settle* for Scott. I chose him, wisely and sensibly and . . . and I made an excellent choice!"

"Hey, if you say so. But if you were my girl, I'd be hanging around your door a little more often than good old Scott. And I'd never let some other guy carry home your sack of rabbit veggies."

"Maybe I wouldn't like Scott hanging around my door all the time," Gwen burst out. "Maybe it would get on my nerves!" Then, appalled at what she'd just said, she hurried on down the River Walk. Robert didn't say anything, but his mocking silence was worse than actual words.

"Too much togetherness isn't good for anybody," she argued. "People need space. Lots of space. If you're part of a couple, you have to remember that. It's the only way to maintain a healthy relationship."

"Maybe you're right, Gwennie. Best way to get along with a man is not to see him. No fights that way, no misunderstandings. No chance for that special someone to get on your nerves."

The more Gwen tried to extricate herself from this conversation, the deeper she sank. Keeping her mouth clamped shut, she veered off the River Walk toward the street where she lived. Robert seemed perfectly content to let the conversation die, but he started to whistle. In perfect pitch, he whistled the romantic Spanish ballad they'd just left behind on the river. Gwen shivered, and this time she couldn't blame it on the cool night air. She was picturing Italy and Mexico all rolled into one, and she knew she had to reach the safety of her house so she could start thinking clearly again.

At last she came to the green picket fence bordering her yard. Her Victorian bungalow seemed to greet her, the front porch spread wide on either side of the door like open arms. There was still so much work to be done on the house—shingles to replace, shutters to paint, cracked windows to repair. But Gwen knew all the work would be worth the effort.

Now she let herself in at the gate and reached out to take her sack of vegetables from Robert. "I'm sure Whiskers will be very grateful to you," she said. "Good night."

He held on to the sack. "I carried this stuff all the way here. Seems like I ought to get a chance to meet the rabbit."

Gwen tapped her fingers on the fence. "Beltramo, we've just spent the entire day together in a kitchen that's way too small for the both of us. Don't you think we ought to give each other a break?"

"I'm curious about this rabbit. But as soon as I meet him, I'm out of here."

Gwen knew exactly what Robert was trying to do—drive her crazy during off-hours, along with everything else. She could hear the laughter in his voice; he was enjoying himself far too much. He was no doubt capable of standing here all night with that sack of vegetables, thinking up new ways to torment her. It would probably be better to let him see the rabbit and be done with it. Gwen let Robert in through the gate and led him around the side of the house. The rabbit hutch was in the backyard. She opened the screened door of the hutch, and Whiskers hopped out.

Whiskers was a big plump rabbit with a patchwork coat of silky fur, all brown and black and white. Gwen stroked his long floppy ears, but his nose was already quivering in Robert's direction. Robert knelt down beside the rabbit and offered him a carrot. Whiskers began nibbling contentedly. Usually the rabbit was leery of strangers, but he seemed to take to Robert with no problem at all.

"Maybe he likes you because you brought him food," Gwen said. "He's never this relaxed around anyone but me."

"Maybe he just likes my personality. Would that be so hard for you to accept, Gwennie?"

"Darn it, you seem to be taking over everything in my life—my restaurant, my employees and now my rabbit. Forget it. I have to draw the line somewhere. The only reason Whiskers is paying any attention to you is because you're plying him with food. He's a munch-mouth. I've been thinking of putting him on a diet, but I just haven't had the heart to do it yet. He loves to eat."

Robert rustled around in the sack, ready to oblige Whiskers with more food. "How'd you end up with a rabbit for a pet? Why not a dog or a parakeet or a goldfish?"

Gwen fiddled with the latch on the hutch door. Things were starting to feel just a little too companionable right now, the December sky a glitter of stars over the backyard, Whiskers happily devouring a lettuce leaf from Robert Beltramo's hand. Gwen didn't want to be as amenable as her rabbit, but she found herself beginning to relax with Robert, too.

"It happened not so long after I bought this house last year," she said. "I woke up one morning and discovered a rabbit on my front porch. There he was, just sitting. I couldn't figure out where on earth he'd come from. None of the neighbors knew anything about him, and nobody answered the notices I put up about a lost rabbit. So, I named him Whiskers and let him chew up my garden. No one's ever claimed him and I'm beginning to suspect no one ever will. I guess the two of us belong together."

Robert fed Whiskers another lettuce leaf. "It figures, Gwennie. A rabbit nobody else seems to want... It's just like this rundown house and my grouchy dad. You take on lost causes."

Gwen should have known better than to let her guard down around the man. He knew exactly how to needle her. "Listen, a lot of things may seem like lost causes to *you*. But maybe that's because you don't know how to look below the surface." Gwen coaxed Whiskers back into his hutch with a carrot, then faced Robert. "Whiskers is a perfectly respectable rabbit, the best pet you could imagine. And your father had a good heart underneath all the grouchiness. Not to mention the fact that someday this house...this house is going to be the best darn home around!"

"Touched a nerve, didn't I?" Robert said mildly. "I know what it is. You're beginning to question your judgment. You're beginning to wonder what kind of boyfriend you picked, and that makes you wonder about everything else. For all you know, your rabbit is going to gobble up everything in sight and your house is going to fall down around your ears. Kind of scary, isn't it?"

Gwen knew he was trying to provoke her and having a good time doing it, too. Unfortunately she fell right in with his plans—she got provoked.

"Come on," she said. "I'm going to show you something. I'm going to show you just how good my judgment really is." She strode to her back door, unlocked it and ushered Robert inside. Flipping on the light, she gestured proudly at her small scullery. "Look at this—notice the details. Those ceiling beams are as sound as the day they were put in. The floor is good sturdy pine, and the sink is real china. Original brass fixtures, too." Gwen turned on one of the spigots to demonstrate its superb action. The pipes immediately began to rattle in protest, making a frightful sound like the clatter of old bones.

Gwen hastily turned off the faucet. "That's a minor plumbing problem," she said when she saw the grin starting on Robert's face. She led him straight through the kitchen to the front parlor. "Okay, take a look at *this,*" she instructed. "One whole section of original wallpaper—over eighty years old—in perfect condition. All these wonderfully carved bookshelves are built right into the wall. And what about the oak mantelpiece? That alone is worth the mortgage payment.''

Robert wandered around the room, examining everything she pointed out, but he didn't seem particularly impressed. Gwen got down to basics now. She swung one of the doors open and shut.

"There, you see? A perfect fit to the frame. That's because every surface in this place is a hundred percent level.'' Next she tapped one of the walls. "Listen to that—solid as anything. No termites here, I can guarantee it.''

Robert had stopped in front of her Christmas tree and was eyeing the pinecones she'd nestled among the branches. He didn't appear the least bit awed by the house's virtues.

"I've just proved to you that this house was a fantastic buy,'' Gwen said. "I was smart to grab it up when I did. So you see, Beltramo, I *do* trust my own judgment. That goes for the house—and the fiancé!''

Robert glanced around, rubbing his jaw thoughtfully. "Speaking of your boyfriend, why don't you have any pictures of the guy? I think that's the way it's supposed to work. You get engaged to someone, and next thing you know you've got big framed photographs of the person sprouting on the mantel, the dresser—everywhere. It even gets a little embarrassing, I hear.''

"Of course I have a picture of Scott—'' she glanced around the room herself ''—somewhere. Why wouldn't I have a picture?''

But there wasn't any picture. There were red and green Christmas candles in pewter candlesticks, three ceramic wise men clustered on a shelf, a desk with an ancient typewriter, two old armchairs with flowered chintz slipcovers, a Victorian curio cabinet waiting to be refinished, a framed sampler, several prints of rustic country scenes—but not one photograph of Scott. Gwen hated admitting that Robert was right.

Now Robert prodded one of the Christmas-tree ornaments, a miniature china cat with a red silk bow around its neck. The china cat danced back and forth. Robert smiled.

"Gwennie, seems like you're determined to make this engagement of yours the most unromantic thing around. I have to hand it to you—you're doing a good job."

Gwen stared at him, realizing what she'd done. She'd actually allowed Robert Beltramo into her house, giving him an opportunity to be more irksome than ever. She knew she ought to get rid of him, but somehow she couldn't resist the urge to defend herself. She began pacing the fringed carpet.

"Beltramo, I'm going to tell you *exactly* how I feel about romance. You asked for it, so here goes. I grew up in a very unromantic family. My mother and father were pleasant to each other, nothing more. They were decent parents, but they just... they just didn't seem very passionate about each other." Gwen paused and looked at Robert. He was taking all this in with a judicious expression on his face. He seemed quite relaxed, standing there next to the Christmas tree. Gwen, however, couldn't relax. She started pacing again. And talking.

"I always told myself I wasn't going to end up like my parents. I swore I was going to have passion in my life. I was so excited when I moved away from Houston, when I came to San Antonio for college. I thought anything could happen here. I thought I was going to find all the excitement and romance my parents never had." Gwen took a deep breath.

"Go on," he said. "Or maybe I can guess the rest of it. You were looking for romance in San Antonio, but you never found it. You met too many guys who were jerks, and—"

"I can tell my own story, darn it." Gwen frowned at him. "I dated enough men of all types to realize that maybe my parents had it right. After all these years, they're still together and they're still friends. So what if they don't get starry-eyed about each other and all that nonsense? Other things are far more important."

"Is that what you and Scott are, Gwennie? Friends?"

Gwen twisted her ring. She couldn't understand why Robert made her question every single aspect of her relationship with Scott.

"I've never thought of it exactly that way. But, yes, of course we're friends. We must be friends... For crying out loud, would you leave that poor tree alone?"

Robert obligingly returned a pinecone to its proper place among the branches. But that only left him free to wander over to the bookshelves.

"Hmm. Quite a collection you have here. All the poems of Elizabeth Barrett Browning, *Wuthering Heights,* everything, it appears, all the Brontës wrote...*Anna Karenina*... You notice a theme, Gwennie? These are all love stories, one way or another. We're talking a shelf crammed full of romance here. In fact, we're talking major romance."

Gwen flushed. "I studied nineteenth-century literature in college. That's why I have all those books."

Robert pulled out *Pride and Prejudice* and began turning the pages. He gave one of his maddening chuckles. "Anybody who owns a complete set of Jane Austen's novels is a hard-core romantic. Now I really understand what's going on with you, Gwendolyn. You only *think* you've given up on romance. But underneath all your so-called sensible decisions about this Scott guy, Jane Austen and all the Brontës are telling you to kick up your heels. Maybe you should listen to them before it's too late."

Gwen had had enough. She strode over to Robert and firmly put *Pride and Prejudice* back on the shelf where it belonged. "We'll just have to continue this fascinating discussion about literature some other time. Good night, Beltramo."

"You said I should be reading some Dickens. You said it'd be good for me. Your shelves are full of Dickens."

She grabbed *A Christmas Carol* off the shelf and smacked it into his hand. "There. Maybe that'll get you in the right spirit."

He balanced the book on his palm, looking pleased. "I seem to remember a love story in here somewhere, too. Something about Scrooge and a pretty girl, way back when he was young. Yep, seems even Scrooge had some romance in him."

"For the last time, I don't want any romance in my life. I want Scott!"

Robert was solemn as he gazed back at Gwen. "If you were really sure about this Scott, I wouldn't be here right now, would I?"

His question lingered on the air, unanswered. Suddenly Gwen was too aware of the pounding of her heart. She crossed her arms tightly, but that didn't do anything to stop her pulse from racing. Somehow she found her gaze traveling to Robert's mouth. He had a sensuous expressive mouth....

Still holding *A Christmas Carol* in one hand, Robert reached out to Gwen and clasped her fingers in his. Then he led her across the room to the graceful arch between the parlor and kitchen. He stopped right beneath the arch.

"Mistletoe," he said when Gwen looked at him in puzzlement. Too late she remembered that she had, indeed, hung a ball of mistletoe in a spot right above her head. Robert bent his own head toward her. And then he kissed her, his lips as gentle and teasing as a cool flurry of snow. Gwen didn't resist. She didn't protest. Instead, she placed a hand on his chest, running her fingers over the soft cloth of his shirt, breathlessly savoring the taste of his mouth.

It was Robert who ended the kiss. He stepped back, his eyes alight with the humor she'd already come to know too well.

"See you tomorrow, Gwennie," he murmured. And then he left, taking *A Christmas Carol* with him as he let himself out the front door. She could hear him whistling cheerfully as he went down the path toward the street.

Gwen stood under the mistletoe for another long moment. Such a confusion of emotions swirled inside her that she couldn't move. Why in heaven's name had she let Robert Beltramo kiss her? Even more disturbing, why had she kissed him back? She was engaged to be married! And she was a very loyal person. Scott deserved better than this from her. He deserved a whole lot better. If only Robert's kiss hadn't been quite so delicious...

At last Gwen wrenched herself from underneath the dratted mistletoe. She plunked down in one of the chintz armchairs and stared at the big diamond sparkling on her finger. She was angry and disgusted with herself. It was obvious that Robert hadn't taken that kiss seriously. He'd surely meant it as one more way to provoke her—as everything he'd said tonight had been yet another way to put her off balance. He seemed to thrive on doing that: vexing her, irritating her, annoying the heck out of her.

Gwen looked at her Christmas tree. She could've sworn that the ornaments were still dancing from Robert's touching them. And she could no longer deny the truth. Robert Beltramo had cleverly touched a nerve with *her.* Ever since she'd met him, her vague unease about marrying Scott had sprung into full-fledged doubt. She couldn't ignore it, not if she truly wanted to make a sensible decision.

Somehow she had to sort out all this emotional turmoil by Christmas Eve. She needed the deadline; she welcomed it. It would force her to confront all her feelings about Scott. But there was one small problem. No—make that one huge problem—Robert Beltramo's continued presence in her life. She knew he'd keep trying to stir up her confusion, instead of allowing her to resolve it in a calm and rational manner. With him around, she'd never be able to see Scott clearly. She'd keep thinking about the taste of Robert's lips on her own. . . .

Gwen pressed both hands against her flushed cheeks. She closed her eyes. "It's only until Saturday," she told herself. "Saturday night Robert Beltramo will be out of the restaurant—and out of my life!"

Right now, she needed to believe that more than anything.

CHAPTER FIVE

"CLAUDINE, WHAT ON EARTH are you doing?" Gwen stopped in midstride on her way through the dining area. Claudine was crouched in the middle of the floor, fiddling with her feet.

"I'm pumping up my shoes, Gwen," she explained. "See, these are the basketball shoes that R.B. recommended. They're so-o-o comfie, and they've helped me nail my jump shot. And there's a special way to pump them full of air. R.B. says if I do that, I stand a good chance of being able to dunk the ball. And R.B. says—"

"Please, no more." Gwen scowled at Claudine's flashy shoes with their bright yellow stripes. "Those aren't the only things full of air in this place lately."

Claudine flexed her feet, openly admiring her pumped-up toes. Then she adjusted the daffodil-yellow sweatband that set off her red hair so well. "Really, Gwen, it's too bad you won't join the Beltramo Buccaneers. R.B. was absolutely right. Basketball promotes employee-employer camaraderie, not to mention the fact that it's good for overall cardiovascular fitness. R.B. says..."

Before she had to listen to any more, Gwen escaped into her small office and banged the door shut. She'd

be rich if she had a nickel for every time Claudine had
uttered the phrase "R.B. says." Even Jeremy had once
been heard to mumble, "R.B. says..." All of a sudden Robert Beltramo had turned into *the* authority on
life. And both Claudine and Jeremy could be found
out back of the restaurant at any spare moment of the
day, dribbling a basketball between their legs and
around their backs. It was driving Gwen nuts.

She glanced at her watch. Nine forty-five Saturday
night, central standard time. In precisely fifteen minutes it would all be over. She only had to hold on fifteen more minutes, and the bet with Robert would be
off. Maybe he'd been driving *her* nuts this week, but
she'd demonstrated an ability to return the favor.
She'd made the pleasurable discovery that a messy
kitchen truly disturbed Robert—he liked his surroundings neat and organized. The past few days
Gwen had surpassed her own ability to cook exuber-
antly, creatively...messily. It had been a most satis-
fying endeavor.

Now Gwen surveyed her cramped office, made
more cramped still by the intrusion of a new desk, a
computer and a fax machine. Robert had wasted no
time in trying to take over this room, as well. His desk
and Gwen's squared off against each other like two
lumbering beasts about to charge into battle. Gwen
squeezed around them and was about to sit down
when she saw the bright red shirt flung across her
chair. It wasn't just any shirt; it was a basketball jersey. Gwen picked the thing up and read what was em-
blazoned in obnoxious yellow letters across the back:
GWENDOLYN. And beneath that: #33.

Was there no limit to what Robert would do? She wadded up the jersey in both hands and considered hurling it into the trash. Then an excellent idea occurred to her. She tossed the jersey onto her desk and headed for the supply closet. The office was now so crowded she couldn't open the closet door all the way, but she managed to rummage around inside and find the box she was looking for. Hauling it out, she quickly got to work, humming Christmas carols to herself.

A short time later Gwen was sitting peacefully at her desk, adding and subtracting figures in her account ledger. Robert came striding into the office and brought himself up short. He glanced around with a frown. A miniature Santa Claus was perched on top of his computer, a border of Christmas lights along his desk flashed merrily on and off, a big pinecone wreath adorned his chair, and every other available surface was draped with tinsel.

"What's this?" he muttered, peeling silver tinsel from his in-and-out basket. Gwen felt she'd done a quick and comprehensive job of decorating; she'd divided a clump of tinsel evenly between the "in" half of the basket and the "out" half.

"I decided you needed to get some Christmas spirit, Beltramo. You've brought in all this fancy office equipment, but I haven't seen you produce one single gingerbread man or candy cane. It's the holiday season, after all."

Robert grimaced as he removed the wreath from his chair. Then he sat down, swinging his feet onto the desk among all the tinsel. He wore jeans and scuffed

cowboy boots of tooled black leather. Texas, those
boots said. After only a week or so in San Antonio,
Robert seemed to be settling right back into Texas.
When he spoke next, his voice came out with more
than his usual touch of a drawl.

"Maybe I'm already in the spirit, Gwennie. I made
sure we got red basketball jerseys, didn't I? That's a
Christmas color for you. Those Rough Riders will really be able to see us coming."

Gwen poked at the jersey still wadded up on a corner of her desk. "What I'd really like to see is *you* going, Robert. Why don't you admit you want to go?
The week is up and you probably can't tolerate my
messiness a second longer. Sell your half of the restaurant to me and we'll both be happy."

Robert stretched his arms and clasped his hands
behind his head. "No chance, Gwendolyn. It's time
for you to sell, not me. But don't worry—I'll still let
you be on my basketball team." He grinned engag-
ingly.

Gwen sighed. "This could get just plain ridiculous.
I don't want to spend the rest of my life sprinkling
flour on the floor and throwing spaghetti at the walls
to drive you crazy. And I don't want to go on having
you drive *me* crazy with your basketball and your re-
marks about how to improve my tortellini soup and
my lasagna noodles and my Italian meatballs. Sell out,
Robert!"

He assumed one of his thoughtful expressions, the
kind Gwen had learned not to trust because they were
usually followed by a zinger. She tensed—and sure
enough, a few seconds later, the zinger came.

"I know what the problem is," he said. "You're engaged, Gwennie, but your boyfriend doesn't occupy your mind enough. If you were thinking about him all the time, you wouldn't have any energy left over to worry about me."

Gwen tapped her pencil against the account ledger. She watched the Christmas lights blink on and off, on and off. "Believe me, Robert, as soon as you're out of this restaurant, I'll spend a whole lot more time thinking about Scott. But first things first."

"So where is he tonight? Out of town again?"

Gwen tapped her pencil a little harder. "He came back during the middle of the week for a few days. But, yes, he's out of town again."

"Too bad I missed him." Robert gestured at his computer. "Maybe he could sell me some good programs for this machine. Why didn't you bring him into the restaurant?"

"That's the last thing I'm going to do as long as you're around. I am not going to introduce you to my fiancé."

"Why not? Maybe Scott and I would get along just fine."

She bent over the account ledger. She didn't want to see Scott and Robert together. She didn't want to start comparing the two of them when they were side by side. She didn't want to start thinking that Robert was more attractive, more energetic, more dynamic....

She threw down her pencil. "There's no reason for you to meet Scott," she grumbled. "I'm sure the two of you have nothing in common. And if you want programs for your computer, go back to New York for them."

Robert idly punched one of his computer keys. "Maybe you're upset because old Scott left you alone on a Saturday night. If you can't get a date even when you're engaged, that's rough."

Gwen picked up her pencil again and almost snapped it in two. "Dammit, I'm not upset. I like being alone on a Saturday night. I'd like to be alone right now. I'd like—" Gwen stopped. There was the laughter in his eyes again. Why couldn't she ever remember that the man thrived on provoking her? Why did she continually give him the satisfaction?

He pulled his computer keyboard toward him and started tapping away. "Can't understand why you don't have one of these machines," he said. "After all, your boyfriend sells computer programs."

"I'm thinking about buying a computer, of course. Just haven't gotten around to it yet."

"I think it's all subconscious with you, Gwennie. It's probably a real inconvenience, not having a computer to keep your accounts. But you resist buying one because deep down it's a way to resist Scott. As long as you don't have any of his computer software in your life, you're not genuinely committed to the guy."

She erased a figure in her account book very studiously. "That's the most ridiculous thing I've ever heard. You're way off base this time."

"Bet old Scott's tried to sell you some of his software, hasn't he? And you've turned him down. You've turned down your own fiancé."

This time when Gwen erased a figure, she almost wore a hole in the page. "How could I possibly buy any of his software when I don't own a computer?"

Robert smiled. "Exactly my point. No computer, no software . . . no Scott."

Gwen gave up entirely trying to balance her accounts. "For your information, Scott is very much a part of my life. Just because I refused to buy his dratted software . . ." She was always saying too much around Robert. She took a deep breath and started again. "Let me tell you how it is, Beltramo. I want Scott in my life, and you out of it."

"Deal," he said softly, swinging his feet down and leaning across his desk. "Gwennie, sign those papers my lawyers prepared and it'll all be over. You can go sailing off to your quiet, unromantic and uneventful marriage without another thought about me. Sounds tempting, doesn't it?"

Gwen couldn't answer for a moment. She chewed the end of her pencil, struggling with this vision of her future that Robert had presented. Quiet, uneventful . . . Could it be that her marriage to Scott would actually be that? Yet that was one of the reasons she'd agreed to marry him. She'd been yearning for placidity after the turmoil of her unsuccessful relationships with other men.

"There are all different types of excitement in life," she declared. "Just because two people know how to get along doesn't mean their lives will be uneventful. Or boring . . ." Gwen's voice trailed off. She couldn't seem to get a good argument going right now. She gazed at Robert, thinking that life would never be boring with *him* around. He had too much fun stirring up trouble, especially where Gwen was concerned. He seemed determined to turn her life upside down and to make her question everything about herself. Energy, motion, excitement—that was Robert, all right. He was like a Texas tornado, sweeping through her life, leaving everything in shambles.

Gwen realized she was spending far too much time gazing at Robert, noting how his dark wavy hair seemed to express all his vibrant energy, how his mouth curved in sensual humor. She remembered how he had kissed her that night.... Gwen slammed her account book shut and made a supreme effort to concentrate on anything but the memory of Robert's lips on hers.

"Beltramo, let's get back to the subject, okay?"

"The restaurant," he said helpfully. Now his gaze was lingering on *her* mouth.

Gwen touched her lips distractedly. "Right. The restaurant. I'm not signing those papers."

Robert watched her for another moment. Then he stood up, shaking his head. "I can see you're a stubborn woman, Gwendolyn. You're not going to give in. Plan A didn't work—having my lawyers make you those generous offers. Now it looks like Plan B didn't work, either—engaging in our little battle of aggravation this past week. There's no other choice. We'll have to move on to Plan C."

Gwen didn't like the sound of this; she didn't like it at all. But Robert seemed happy. He stood there with his hands tucked into the back pockets of his jeans, gazing off into some unknown distance. He smiled, and that smile gave Gwen a sense of foreboding.

"Beltramo, what are you up to this time? I've had enough of your plans."

"This is a good one, Gwennie. Real good. Can't wait to get started. Got any tape?"

"What?" Gwen's sense of foreboding was growing stronger by the second. And Robert seemed to be gearing up even more than usual. He rocked on the heels of his cowboy boots, as if the office was too small to confine him anymore.

"Tape, Ferris," he repeated. He started glancing around purposefully, no doubt getting ready to ransack the place. Once Robert had his mind set on something, he went after it. Gwen rummaged in her Christmas-ornament box and found a roll of masking tape. She tossed it at him and he caught it effortlessly. Then he went striding into the dining area, and Gwen had no choice but to follow.

Claudine and Jeremy had already gone home. The room was swept and clean, fresh tablecloths and silver laid, but Robert started disturbing things. He began pushing tables to one side or the other in an obscure arrangement only he understood.

"You know, you come across as such an organized person," Gwen said. "You like everything neat and orderly—but you don't seem to mind disrupting other people's order. It isn't fair."

"Wait till you see this, Gwennie. You're going to like Plan C."

"Darn it, do you always have a plan?"

He paused for a moment to glance at her, as if surprised she'd even ask such a question. "If one plan doesn't get results, you just have to come up with another one. You never get anywhere by brooding about the things that didn't work out in the past. You move on to something else." With that, Robert continued pushing tables around.

Gwen sat down at one of the tables and watched him. No one could ever accuse Robert Beltramo of standing still and brooding about past failures. In fact, she suspected the word "failure" wasn't even part of his vocabulary. But Gwen didn't know whether she should admire him for that or run for the nearest cover.

He crossed to the table where Gwen was sitting and pulled it clean away from her. She folded her arms and planted her feet on the floor, remaining seated exactly where she was. Robert walked around her, as if getting ready to heft up her chair and carry her off to a location of his own choosing. Gwen twisted her head and glared at him. At last he gave a slight shrug and went to the other end of the room with his roll of masking tape.

Crouching, he began marking a line along the floor with the tape. Deftly he worked his way toward Gwen again, his line of tape leading right to her sneakered feet. Gwen wouldn't have been surprised to see him run the tape up her chair and over her head, but she refused to budge.

"Beltramo, do you mind telling me what it is you're doing?"

He stood and grinned at her. "It's simple. We're going to divide the restaurant straight down the middle, Ferris. I'm going to run one half, and you're going to run the other. It's the best way to handle a fifty-fifty partnership neither one of us wants."

Gwen surveyed what he'd done to the room. He had, indeed, pushed half of the tables to one side and half to the other. And the tape running down the middle of the floor clearly marked the dividing line.

"It won't work," Gwen said flatly. "We'll still drive each other nuts. The place is too small for a crazy gimmick like this."

Robert was already off in another corner of the room, pacing off measurements along the floor. "I haven't finished telling you all of it. We'll only divide the restaurant like this for a couple of weeks—until Christmas, say. The point is to see which one of us makes the most money during that time. And whoever *does* make the most, he or she is the winner."

Gwen leaned down and peeled up a corner of the tape. "Winner of what?" she demanded.

"The restaurant, of course. Whoever pulls in the most profits by Christmas Eve will have the privilege of buying out the other person. It's simple, it's logical, it's fair. Damn, Plan C is good." Sounding inordinately happy, Robert pushed through the swinging door into the kitchen.

Gwen jumped up from her chair and hurried after him. She found him poking his nose into one of the pizza ovens.

"We'll need more equipment," he said, clanging the oven shut. "But that won't be too difficult. I can have

another refrigerator installed here by Monday, and
new ovens by the middle of the week. And we'll operate the dishwasher on a time-share basis." Robert
whipped a small pad out of his shirt pocket, along
with a fountain pen, and started jotting notes.

"For Pete's sake, slow down, Beltramo. I haven't
agreed to any of this yet."

"You'll agree, Gwennie. You'll see that this is the
best way to resolve the bind we're in. You want the
restaurant, I want the restaurant, neither one of us is
willing to compromise—so we'll make it a contest.
We're talking some great publicity potential here."

Gwen propped her elbows on the counter and
rubbed her temples. Robert's enthusiasm seemed to fill
the small kitchen.

"Look, I've been working here since I started college," she said. "I've put so much time and effort and
love into this place. But you're asking me to gamble all
that on the basis of a few weeks' earnings!"

"What other choice do you have? Can you picture
tussling with me over this place indefinitely? The two
of us elbowing for room in this kitchen all the time?
Think about it. We'd never be rid of each other. But
with my plan, in only a few short weeks one of us has
to bow out and leave the other person alone for good."

Gwen rubbed her temples some more. She hated
being in this position, backed into a corner so ex-
pertly by Robert. He made his plan sound persuasive,
the only logical choice left open to her. If she agreed
to this wild idea, she *would* be gambling the restaurant. But she'd also have a good chance of winning the

place for herself once and for all. Oh, it was tempting, all right.

Robert's pen squirted ink over his pad. "Damn," he muttered, frowning. His fountain pen looked familiar to her—the distinctive gold scrolling, the dark glossy wood of the pen's surface...

"That used to belong to Pop," she said. "For some reason I never figured out, he used to call it his good-luck pen."

Robert turned it around in his fingers. "Thing doesn't even work right, always spitting ink at the wrong time. So much for good luck."

"Why are you bothering with it, then?"

Robert made a restless motion. "It was lying around the house. I must have picked it up by accident and put it in my pocket."

"Maybe it means something to you," Gwen persisted. "Maybe it's a memento, something to remind you of your father."

Robert's face took on a closed look. "Don't try to read any significance into it. I found the pen, I put it to use. Turned out to be a stupid idea."

Gwen reached across the counter and started re-stacking some custard cups. "You think you have me figured out, Robert, but I'm starting to figure *you* out. You come charging back to San Antonio with all these plans about taking over the restaurant, only that's not why you're really here. You're looking for something, I think, something to do with your father. You said it yourself the other day. You said your father died, and that's when you knew something was missing in your life."

Robert jammed the cap back on the pen. "I was talking about challenge. I knew I needed some kind of new challenge. So I did the right thing—I took action."

"Maybe taking action isn't the right thing to do. Instead of rushing in here and trying to take over my restaurant, maybe you should've stopped to find out what's really bothering you."

Robert surveyed her mockingly. "Okay, Ferris. You have it all figured out. What's really bothering me?"

She gazed at him across the counter. "I don't know anything about what happened between you and your father when you were growing up. But I'd say you came back to San Antonio to resolve it somehow... to make peace with your father. Only you'll never make peace as long as you're covering things up with all this motion and activity. Trying to take over the restaurant is just a way for you to ignore the real issue."

Robert's features had tightened still further. "I get it. I'm supposed to conveniently leave the restaurant to you while I sort out all those deep hidden conflicts about my dad."

She grabbed one of her Christmas dish towels and swiped at a spot on the counter. "I was just trying to... to help, that's all."

"The way you help your customers? I've watched you this week, Gwendolyn. You always end up sitting down with the patrons out there, listening to their problems. You act like you're fascinated by every detail they tell you. Lord, the rapt expression you get on your face when they're talking to you—they probably think you can solve all their problems, not just listen to them. But I'm not one of those customers. Don't try to look inside my head."

Gwen yanked up the sleeves of her polo shirt. "I know what I'd find if I did look inside your head," she snapped. "Basketball brains! You're just using this place, Robert. You're using it to avoid the truth about you and your father. Well, I won't let you do it. I won't agree to Plan C or Plan D or any other cockamamy plan you happen to hatch while you're refusing to confront your own feelings." Gwen stopped, out of breath and out of sorts. She and Robert went on facing each other across the counter. Robert looked grim and determined, implacable.

"We're going to make a bargain," he said quietly. "We're going to divide this place down the middle and see who really knows how to run it better. And on Christmas Eve we'll find out who's going to end up with the restaurant once and for all."

"You're basing the whole contest on who makes the most money. That doesn't measure customer satisfaction, or what kind of food is served, or—"

"Right. And it doesn't measure how many times you sit down with your customers at dessert to hear their life stories. It's not supposed to measure those things. It's just supposed to show who's the better businessperson."

"It takes a lot of different skills to make a business succeed," she argued. "Maybe I know some things you don't, in spite of all your experience in New York."

"Show me," he said. "That's what this is all about. Your chance to show you can do better than me."

Gwen shook out her dish towel and gazed at the cheerful pattern of old-fashioned sleighs piled high with Christmas gifts. This was supposed to be a season of joy and good wishes. It wasn't supposed to be a time of battle and rivalry. And it sure wasn't supposed to be a time when you worried about whether your restaurant would survive intact to see the New Year.

"If I agree to your plan," she said, "Pop's Restaurant will never be the same again—even if I do win the contest. I don't want things to change."

"Everything changes," Robert said harshly. "You should know that as much as anyone. You're the person who turned this place into one big family hour, treating the customers like they're all your favorite relatives. It wasn't like that when I was growing up, trust me. But now things are going to change again. They've already started to change." Robert drew his eyebrows together as he studied the fountain pen in his hand. He seemed about to throw it away, but then he tucked it back into his pocket. He shut his notepad on the splatter of ink, and crammed that back into his pocket, too.

Robert acted, she thought, as if he could put away all his bitter feelings about his father as easily as he'd put away that pen and pad. Now he glanced around the kitchen again, his air of purpose back full force.

"It's going to take a little work, dividing the place," he said. "But in a day or two we'll be ready to start.

And we'll begin publicizing the contest right away, of course. We can draw all sorts of customers who'll come just for curiosity's sake."

Gwen winced at the thought of curiosity seekers thronging to homey, friendly Pop's Restaurant. She watched as Robert poked through the cabinets, no doubt mentally dividing them in half, too. But then he turned and gave Gwen a faint smile.

"What's it to be, Gwennie—yes or no? Why don't you try to prove to me that your way of doing business is the best? Prove to me that treating your customers like long-lost family is actually good for business. If you do that, I'll be the first to applaud you."

Oh, he wanted a challenge, all right. He wanted a game, and he'd just tossed the ball to Gwen. Her move was next. Things had already started to change around here; there was no turning back, and she knew it. And maybe Robert Beltramo *did* need her to prove something to him. Maybe he needed it badly. Besides, Gwen had never turned down a challenge in her life. She wasn't going to turn down this one. She'd gamble on her ability to run this place the way it needed to be run—and she'd win.

"You're on, Robert," she said coolly. "We'll divide things straight down the middle, and we'll find out which one of us really knows this business."

Robert's smile turned to a wide grin. "Here's to Christmas Eve," he said, raising one of the custard cups in a mock salute.

Gwen raised her own custard cup. "Yes, to Christmas Eve." Because that was the night when it seemed everything about Gwen's life would be decided—everything that mattered at all.

CHAPTER SIX

THWACK! THWACK! BANG! Thwack! Tap, tap, bang!

Gwen moaned and clapped her hands over her ears. The racket on Robert's side of the restaurant had been going on nonstop for two days now. What was he up to over there? Gwen couldn't tell because huge opaque sheets of plastic hung all the way down the middle of the restaurant. Now and then she could see vague shadowy figures moving back and forth behind the plastic, like the ghosts of Christmas past, present and future. Gwen was beginning to suspect that Robert had hired a whole army of contractors to remodel his side of the restaurant. It sounded as if he was having the entire place torn down and then rebuilt.

Thwack! Bang! Thwack!

Gwen contemplated investing in a pair of ear plugs, or maybe a soundproof helmet. She escaped outside and found a bit of relief from the noise. But even here, in the outdoor eating area, one of those wretched plastic sheets divided Robert's side from Gwen's. On her side, the wrought-iron patio tables were clustered in an inviting arrangement, as usual. But on Robert's side . . . well, what *was* going on over there? Now she heard bizarre scraping sounds. Screech! Crunch! Screech!

Gwen inched her way toward the plastic sheet, trying to see through. No success. Now she slid toward the end of the sheet, intending merely to take one quick glance around it. She started to peer—and bumped smack into Robert Beltramo. He reached out to steady her, his hands strong and warm.

"Whoa, Gwendolyn. Looking for someone? Your boyfriend, maybe? Sorry to tell you he's not over here. He's out of—"

"I know very well Scott's out of town again." She backed away hastily from Robert's touch. "I just think I ought to see what you're doing. It sounds like things are getting way out of hand."

Robert smiled. "The unveiling's tomorrow, Gwennie. You'll have to wait until then. Besides, anticipation makes everything just a little more enticing."

"Anticipation, my foot," Gwen muttered. She went to lean against the railing that overlooked the river. It was another warm sunny December day—a cheerful day. But in spite of the pleasant weather, Gwen felt on edge. This scheme of Robert's was definitely running away with itself.

Robert came to stand at the railing beside her. She tried not to let her gaze stray toward him, but it was impossible. This morning Robert looked especially good. He wore jeans and a striped rugby shirt that emphasized his broad chest. A tool belt was slung over his hips like a holster. Instead of a six-shooter, however, Robert's belt packed a claw hammer, a hand drill, several screwdrivers and a tape measure.

"So you're getting in on the action yourself," Gwen remarked. "You're probably tearing down the walls personally."

Robert patted his hammer. "I can't just stand around and watch everyone else do the work. Where's the enjoyment in that?"

"No one would ever accuse you of just standing around," Gwen said dryly. She gazed into the dark water of the river. It seemed to her that Robert was like the river, mysterious and exotic, with hidden currents never at rest. Oh, damn. Did she have to see Robert Beltramo wherever she looked?

As always, Robert was brimming with ideas, but today he didn't share them with Gwen. He merely whipped out that pad of his and began jotting more notes. It made Gwen uneasy; everything he wrote down probably heralded a change in *her* life. For all she knew, he was outlining a plan to turn the restaurant into a five-story luxury boat ready to go floating down the river. She craned her neck to see the pad, but Robert's handwriting was so vigorous and energetic she couldn't decipher anything from this angle. Her task was also made difficult by the fact that Robert was once again using his father's fountain pen. It left little splotches of ink on the paper at regular intervals. Robert caught Gwen studying his writing. He frowned, recapped the pen and stuffed it into his tool belt.

"So, Gwendolyn. I get the impression you're making a few changes on your own side."

She nudged the toe of her sneaker against the railing. "Only a few minor alterations. I'm just sprucing things up a little."

"Thought you wanted everything to stay exactly the same in this place."

She glanced at him sharply. "I'm not changing the spirit of Pop's Restaurant, that's what's important. I've always had ideas about how to improve the place—there's nothing wrong with that. Pop would understand."

Robert looked interested. "So you're saying it's a good thing we're doing now, making all our changes."

"I'm not saying that at all. I don't have a good feeling in the least about the racket you're making on your side. Who knows what you're doing? But my changes...my changes are fine." Fact of the matter was, she'd started to wonder if *she* wasn't getting a little carried away. Her own vision for the restaurant had seemed to blossom once Robert's Plan C went into effect. It was as if all her secret dreams for the place had started coming to life; she hadn't been able to resist them. It was a disturbing phenomenon, and she certainly didn't want Robert to know about it. Ever since she'd met him, more and more things about her life seemed to be spinning out of control. Every day it was worse—every day more hidden longings stirred inside her. Now those longings were spilling out, changing how she viewed the restaurant, changing how she wanted the place to look. What on earth would change next?

"I hate having the restaurant closed down this long," she said. "We've never done anything like this before, and I'm sure all my customers are feeling very displaced.''

"You focus too much on that small group of regulars you have. This contest is going to stimulate a lot of new business. Wait and see what the publicity alone does.''

Gwen sighed. Robert had lost no time in publicizing their contest. He'd taken out newspaper ads, contacted the local television stations and sent Claudine and Jeremy all over town with flyers.

"Wait a minute!'' Gwen exclaimed. "With all this crazed activity, we haven't even discussed what'll happen to Jeremy and Claudine when we open for business again. If the restaurant is divided, they can't work for both of us.''

Robert shrugged, undisturbed. "I'll take Jeremy on my side. You take Claudine.''

"That's making them choose sides. The three of us have been like a family until now.''

"Jeremy's not your kid brother, and Claudine's not your sister. They'll handle the situation just fine.''

"How can you be so matter-of-fact about the whole thing?'' Gwen asked. "In case you haven't noticed, both Jeremy and Claudine think you're the best thing to come along since pita bread. If Claudine works with me, she'll feel unhappy about competing against you.''

Robert shook his head. "Gwennie, if you'd ever come to our basketball practices, you'd know that Claudine is a killer when it comes to competition. She loves it. She'll see this as another game and have a grand time of it. In fact, I think we're all going to have a grand time." His face was alight with that trademark enthusiasm of his.

"*I* don't see this bizarre contest as a game," she protested. But that only brought the familiar laughter shimmering into Robert's amber-brown eyes.

"You don't, Gwennie?" he asked softly. "You don't see the fun of it, the exhilaration? Pitting yourself against me, measuring all the obstacles, doing your damnedest to win..."

Yes, at Robert's words, a wave of exhilaration did sweep through her. She wanted to fight him. "Maybe I will have a little fun beating you," she declared. "Because that's what's going to happen, Beltramo. I know how to run this business, and I'm going to beat your socks off!"

He nodded in obvious pleasure. "That's the spirit, Gwennie. It's just that kind of gumption I need on my basketball team. This afternoon's our first game against the Rough Riders. Sure you won't join us?"

"No way," she said stubbornly.

"I'm saving your jersey for you, just in case." He smiled at her, and with that, he and his tool belt vanished behind the plastic sheet again.

EARLY IN THE AFTERNOON Robert, Claudine and Jeremy all trekked off to the basketball court in their bright red jerseys and pumped-up shoes. Gwen was left to listen to the pound of hammers and the whine of electric drills coming from the contractors busy on Robert's side of the restaurant. She tried to put the finishing touches on her own new decorating scheme, but after a few hours she gave up. She couldn't even think with all this noise. And she kept wondering in the most annoying fashion whether or not the Beltramo Buccaneers had trounced the Roosevelt Rough Riders.

Gwen went home along the River Walk, telling herself it was wonderful to have this unexpected leisure time. But it didn't feel wonderful. She was used to working hard at the restaurant six full days a week. On her one day off, she usually ran errands. She wasn't used to leisure, not at all.

At home she wandered out to her tangled winter garden and watched Whiskers hop around in search of unshriveled leaves.

"Whiskers," she said, "I can't believe Robert Beltramo had you eating out of the palm of his hand."

Robert again! Couldn't she keep him out of her thoughts for one second? Gwen stalked into her house. She went to her desk in the parlor, got a notebook and tore out a sheet of paper. Then she wrote in bold capital letters across the top of the page: "SCOTT." Next she drew a line down the middle of the page. On one side she wrote, "Pro," on the other, "Con." This was just what she needed, analyzing Scott in concrete terms. On the "Pro" side, she listed "dependable, hardworking, wants to raise a family, even-tempered, likes my cooking..." Gwen doodled a few random designs on the paper, not sure what to put next. There had to be something else, but for the moment she couldn't think of anything. Very well, perhaps it was time to move to the "Con" side. This category, however, turned out to be even more difficult. What could she write? That Scott didn't have Robert Beltramo's sense of humor, that he didn't have Robert's zest and enthusiasm, Robert's lips that could kiss with all the spicy taste of Italy....

"For crying out loud!" Gwen threw her pencil clear across the room, almost taking down an ornament on the Christmas tree. How was she ever going to be fair to Scott under circumstances like these? She had Robert Beltramo on the brain, that was the problem. She just had to figure out a way to get him off her brain!

Gwen started crumpling her sheet of paper, but then she heard odd noises coming from her front porch. Clack...clack...bang! Goodness, this was almost as bad as being at the restaurant again. Now Gwen folded her crumpled page, stuffed it into the pocket of her polo shirt and went to peer out the window. She found herself gazing at a foot, of all things, a masculine foot wearing a scuffed, black leather cowboy boot as it balanced itself on Gwen's windowsill. She narrowed her eyes, then strode to the front door, swept it open and marched out onto her porch. And here was the owner of the boot, none other than the cause of most of her problems: R.B. himself.

One foot astride the porch railing and the other anchored on the windowsill, Robert was reaching up to the ceiling with a screwdriver, fiddling with the brackets of the porch swing. His body was twisted rather awkwardly, but he managed to retain his balance.

"Hello, there, Gwennie," he said, as if there was nothing unusual about his performing acrobatics on her front porch.

"Beltramo, what are you doing up there? You think you're one of the Flying Wallendas now?"

He went on working away in his awkward position. "The screws are almost all stripped," he said. "No wonder the swing is hanging loose at that end."

"My porch swing is fine."

"Gwennie, you have to think these things through. Suppose one night you and the boyfriend decide to sit out here for a little stargazing. You snuggle up together on the swing, you start swinging, and, next thing you know, whammo. This thing crashes to the floor with both of you in it. What then?"

She was sorely tempted to confiscate all of Robert's screwdrivers. "I can take care of myself, all right? And his name is Scott, not 'the boyfriend.' And I'm not in the habit of snuggling up with him on the porch swing!"

"Hmm. No snuggling. That's pretty unromantic."

Gwen took a deep breath. "That's right. It is unromantic, and that's exactly the way I like it. Now, why are you here?"

"Let's just say I get a lot of enjoyment out of bugging you, Gwendolyn. I had to come over." He loosened another screw, and one whole end of the swing went crashing to the floor. Robert looked regretful. "Besides, the contractors at the restaurant threw me out. Told me not to come back until I was a licensed carpenter. Go figure."

Gwen scowled. "I don't blame them for kicking you out. You were probably driving them crazy with your tool belt and your mania for loosening screws. Except now you're here to annoy me."

"What choice did I have?" he asked solemnly. "The other night I could tell this place needed a lot of work. The boyfriend—Scott, that is—never seems around long enough to do repairs for you. Somebody has to fill in."

She groaned. Robert's threatening to take over the restaurant was bad enough, but now he threatened to take over her house, as well. Here he was, his vibrant presence dominating the porch. After his basketball game he'd changed back into his jeans and rugby shirt, his curling hair damp from a shower. And that tool belt was slung around his hips again. He looked like he was cruising for trouble.

"So, how'd the game turn out?" Gwen couldn't help asking.

"It was close, Gwennie, real close. We lost by three points."

"Too bad," she murmured.

"We'll just have to do better next time. I've already scheduled extra practice sessions. Those parking attendants had better not get too cocky, that's all I can say."

Gwen should've realized that nothing discouraged Robert for long. "That's great," she said. "But I'm really busy. I'm in the middle of something very important."

"I wouldn't want to intrude. Scott back in town, that it?"

She glared at him. "No, he's not back. But he might call me on the phone...or something." Now that Gwen thought about it, she realized Scott rarely called her when he was out of town. She hadn't particularly noticed that before, but Robert made her notice all sorts of new and disturbing things.

Robert jumped easily down from the railing and smiled at her. "Listen, Gwennie, all I need is a step-ladder. I'll have this swing fixed for you in no time."

Once Robert had decided on a project, he went at it full force. Her porch swing would never be the same again. And, Gwen feared, neither would she. But after a moment's hesitation, she went inside the house, found her stepladder and dragged it back out to him. He climbed up on it, loosened the last ceiling bracket, and now the whole swing sprawled on the floor in an ungainly heap of chains.

Gwen sat down on the porch steps, clasping her arms around her knees, and watched Robert work. Whenever he was in motion like this, he seemed in his element. Whistling under his breath, he deftly marked out some measurements on the ceiling. Then he began making new holes, and she found the sound of his hand drill rather pleasing as it bit into the wood, a sort of crunching whisper. It was a pleasant change from the whine of electric drills.

Leaning back against the porch railing, she found tension easing out of her. As sawdust drifted down through the sunlit air like a shower of gold sequins, Gwen half closed her eyes, thinking how companionable these few moments were. Neither she nor Robert spoke, and there didn't seem any need to speak. It was agreeable just to sit here and have a virile competent man making repairs....

Gwen stood up quickly, alarmed at the direction of her thoughts.

When Robert was done remounting the swing, it hung perfectly straight and even looked stronger than before. Surely it would never come crashing down, no matter how many romantic couples snuggled on it.

"Well," Gwen said briskly. "I suppose I appreciate this. And now you're finished with the job."

Robert didn't take her hint. He fished a piece of sandpaper from the back pocket of his jeans and started rubbing the wooden seat of the swing.

"You know what your problem is?" Gwen said. "You don't know how to sit back and enjoy the moment. You always have to be doing something, working on a project or thinking up some new plan to hound innocent people like me. You really ought to learn how to be . . . well, motionless."

Robert brushed off the swing. "Hmm. That does sound good." He plunked himself down in the swing, apparently taking Gwen up on her suggestion.

"That's not exactly what I meant," she began.

"You try it with me. Let's make sure this contraption is safe." Before she could protest, he drew her down beside him on the swing. Her thigh brushed his, but the swing was small and she couldn't scoot away. Gwen clasped her hands in her lap, her heartbeat speeding into a new rhythm. She didn't have any excuse to be sitting here with Robert Beltramo, no excuse at all. She wasn't snuggling, not by any means, but even the light touch of his leg against hers seemed too intimate. Why didn't she simply jump up and break the contact? Her own answer to that question was not reassuring: she wanted to be near Robert. She needed to be near him, that was all.

He pushed his boot against the floor and the swing rocked back and forth. "Works pretty good, doesn't it?" he observed.

"It's...adequate."

"I know what you're thinking. You're thinking old Scott would be jealous if he saw us like this."

Gwen dug a fingernail into her skin. "As a matter of fact, he wouldn't be jealous. He's not that kind of person."

"If you were my girl, I'd be jealous as hell."

"I'm *not* your girl," she retorted. "Which makes this discussion pointless."

"Not at all." He draped one arm casually across the back of the swing. "You should never trust a guy who's not jealous, Gwennie. Remember that."

Gwen pushed her foot against the floor and gave the swing a good rock. "I don't want Scott to be jealous."

"Ah, another bad sign."

"Two rational adults don't need to be tormented by jealousy!"

Robert stretched his arm out a little more and it brushed against Gwen's back. "Every healthy engagement needs a little torment," he remarked.

"What makes you such an authority? Have you ever been engaged?"

Robert seemed to ponder this question. "I guess you could say I came close once. Yep, I came real close."

Gwen turned toward Robert. "So what happened with this woman and your close-engagement?"

"Maybe we just didn't have enough torment between us. No jealousy, no snuggling—nothing."

Gwen saw the laugh lines around his eyes crinkle. "Can't you be serious for once?" she asked. "Why didn't you marry her, Robert? Really."

"Because I wasn't in love with her, and I had the sense to realize that before it was too late."

Gwen tried to move away from Robert's arm, but the swing was too cozy. "I don't think being in love is all it's cracked up to be. I've been in love plenty of times myself—or at least I thought I was in love, and it only made me miserable. I mean, if you're going to be tormented by love, you ought to be able to have some happiness, too!"

"Definitely," Robert said. "Tormented happiness."

Gwen rocked the swing with another vigorous push of her foot. "I don't know why I'm even bothering to talk to you," she grumbled.

"Gwennie, I've figured it out. The problem is that you've never been in real honest-to-goodness love. You're trying to be an expert on something you don't know anything about."

"Well, if you know so much about it..."

"Maybe I don't," he said reflectively. "Maybe I've never really been in love, either. Maybe you and I are just a couple of amateurs here, sharing a porch swing. Pretty sobering, isn't it?"

He was still filled with laughter. She gazed at him, wishing she knew what to believe. Was he telling the truth about never having been in love, or was he merely teasing her again? And why did she care whether or not he'd been in love once or twice or a hundred times?

Back and forth the swing creaked. First Robert would push off with one of his cowboy boots, then Gwen would nudge the floor with the toe of her sneaker. Back and forth...you'd almost think they were a team. Now, that was a laugh. But Gwen couldn't look away from him. His face was close to hers and the blood warmed in her veins, as if she were a kettle and Robert had turned up the heat. And then, the swing rocking gently, Robert bent his head and captured her lips with his.

It was a kiss cloaked in twilight and mystery, a kiss that stirred a dark aching desire somewhere deep inside Gwen. She strained toward Robert, there on the swing, and now he deepened the kiss. It became a kiss of passion and longing and the sweetest torment—

"No," Gwen whispered against Robert's mouth. "No!" She jumped up suddenly and Robert steadied the swing, scraping the heel of his boot against the floor. He didn't say anything and Gwen stood there, distractedly twisting her engagement ring. Too late she realized how hard she was twisting, and the dratted ring flew right off her finger again. It sailed up, the diamond catching a last glint of sunlight, and then it plummeted downward—and Gwen watched in horror as the ring disappeared through one of the cracks between the uneven floorboards. This time, maybe this time, the ring was gone for good!

CHAPTER SEVEN

GWEN DROPPED to her hands and knees, peering down into the crack. She couldn't see a thing. "I've really done it now," she muttered. "Robert, why did you have to go and kiss me like that?"

He knelt beside her. "Look at it this way, Gwennie. If you'd just relaxed and gone on kissing, you'd probably still have your ring."

"If I'd never kissed you in the first place... Oh, forget it! I have to find that ring, do you hear?" As she crouched down still further, squinting into the crack, the piece of paper in her shirt pocket slipped out onto the floor. Robert retrieved it.

"What's this—another attempt at a paper airplane?" Robert started unfolding the crumpled sheet. "Looks like you mauled it."

"How can you think about paper airplanes at a time like this? No, wait, don't read that!" Dismayed, Gwen remembered what she'd written on that sheet. Pieces of her life were always tumbling out of her pockets when she was around Robert! After losing her ring again, she hadn't believed things could get worse. But they were worse, all right.

Robert leaned back against one of the porch pillars and held the paper up toward the fading light. "Tell you the truth, Gwennie, I wasn't going to read this until you got into such a swivet about it just now. Which leads me to believe that, subconsciously, you do want me to read it, and I have no choice but to oblige. Let's see, pros and cons of old Scott..."

She tried to snatch the page away from him, but he dodged her easily. "Beltramo," she said through clenched teeth. "Consciously or subconsciously or *un*consciously, I do not want you to read that."

He started to grin. "I've been right all along. You've had doubts about whether or not to marry this guy. Looks like it's *sayonara*, Scott. Good for you, Gwennie."

She sat down on the floor of the porch and hugged her knees. "I'm not planning to break up with Scott. I'm just trying to...to resolve a few things."

"Guess I'll have to help you out." Robert brought out his father's fountain pen and uncapped it. "You need some cons over here. I can think of plenty of cons. Number one, the guy's not the jealous type. Number two, he's always out of town. On second thought, maybe that's a pro. We don't really want him around now, do we?" Resting the paper against his knee, Robert forcefully jotted on it, leaving a trail of splotchy ink down the page. Gwen watched him, wondering how on earth to stop this nonsense. Every second she was around Robert, her life seemed more and more out of control. He made her feel like she was on a wild roller-coaster ride and didn't know how to get off.

"Here's a pro for Scott," she said. "He'd never try to muscle away my restaurant."

"Afraid that's a con. 'No competitive spirit.' Let's see, what else? 'No romance, doesn't play basketball, doesn't kiss his girlfriend enough—'"

"What makes you think that?" Gwen demanded indignantly.

Robert glanced at her, his eyes dark in the shadows of dusk. "I can tell you don't get kissed enough, Gwendolyn. Believe me, I can tell."

Her face burned, and this time she did snatch the piece of paper away from him. She crumpled it up once and for all and tossed it to the far end of the porch. "It just so happens I've lost my engagement ring, and I'd like to get on with looking for it." She dug her fingers into the crack between the floorboards.

"You'll never find it that way. Of course, something tells me that subconsciously you don't really want to find it—"

"Robert, will you leave my subconscious out of this? I have enough problems!"

"All right, let's do this the organized way. You have a flashlight?"

Gwen was relieved for an excuse to get away from Robert for a few moments. She went through her house, flipping on lights and searching through cluttered drawers. She could've sworn she had a flashlight around here somewhere.

She paused in the middle of poking through a particularly jumbled drawer and stared down, unseeing, at the clutter. What in tarnation made Robert Beltramo think she needed kissing? Just because Scott didn't happen to be the most enthusiastic kisser in the world, just because he never made her heart pound ridiculously the way it did when Robert's lips touched hers ...

Gwen slammed the drawer shut and gave up on finding a flashlight. She found some matches, instead, grabbed her old kerosene lantern from the scullery and strode out to the porch. Robert studied the lantern dubiously.

"Maybe you forgot what century we're in here," he said. "Now and then modern technology comes in handy."

"It works perfectly well." Gwen turned on the kerosene and lit a match. Light flared inside the glass globe—warm, romantic light, when she came to think of it. Gwen frowned at the lantern, but Robert was all energy and purpose now.

"There must be an access panel somewhere that'll let me under the porch. You stay here so you can show me which crack that damn rock fell through. I'll try to find out where it landed." Robert disappeared around the side of the house, and a few moments later wavering beams of light came up through the cracks in the porch floor.

"Any luck?" Gwen asked. She could see that Robert was crawling on his hands and knees in the cramped space. It looked pretty uncomfortable.

"Not yet" came his voice. "Lord, it's like a swamp under here. That ring could've sunk in the mud never to be seen again."

"Don't say that. We have to find it."

"Thought you said old Scott wouldn't be upset by something like this. Thought you said he'd just call his insurance company."

Gwen squinted down through a crack. "That's not the point. The point is, I owe it to Scott to find the ring. He deserves at least that much from me."

"Gwennie, when you start thinking you owe a man something, that's another bad sign. Courtship isn't supposed to be a balance sheet. You should be so loony about the other person that you can't even think about debits or credits. Or pros or cons, for that matter."

Gwen planted a hand on either side of the crack and glared down through it. "Beltramo, I'm going to crawl under there myself and find that diamond."

"I like the sound of that." The lantern light swayed from side to side. "It could get pretty chummy with both of us down here. Now, poke your finger through the crack where the ring fell, so I can get my bearings."

Gwen stuck her fingers between the boards, making a strangled sound of sheer frustration. She knew she must look pretty silly right now, crouched over and arguing with an unseen man under her floorboards. But this whole thing had gone beyond silly. Way beyond.

"You want to talk debits and credits" came Robert's voice, "let me tell you something. After having me swim around in the muck down here, I think you owe *me.*"

She stared suspiciously through the crack. "Hold on. After all the aggravation you've caused me, you should be doing this out of the kindness of your heart."

"I'm as kindhearted as the next guy. But if I ever do find that rock of yours, you'll owe me one heck of a favor."

Gwen didn't like the sound of that at all. "What kind of favor?" she demanded. "I have a bad feeling that you're hatching some new plan, Beltramo—Plan D, or even worse, Plan E."

Odd rustling noises came from under the porch, as if Robert was trying to do somersaults in the cramped space. "Yep, you're really going to owe me for this one. Of course, chances are a million to one I'll ever find it. But if I do—"

Gwen smacked the floorboards. "Okay, okay, I'll do you a favor. Whatever you like. You'll have my undying gratitude. Just find the darned ring!"

"You sure you won't go back on this, Gwennie? You'll do anything I ask?"

"I promise," she said acidly.

"What do you know—found it!"

"Blast it, Beltramo. You set me up," she accused. "You probably found it right off, but decided to torment me."

"I keep telling you that you need more torment in your life." Robert poked the muddy diamond ring up through the crack. Gwen snatched it and slipped it back onto her finger, but she didn't feel any better. She certainly didn't feel any more in control. Robert crawled out from under the porch and came up the steps, the lantern bobbing in his hand. He looked muddy but pleased.

"Pay-up time, Ferris. You promised me a favor, and I'm here to collect."

She folded her arms and kept a wary stance on the porch. "I'm convinced you extracted that promise under false pretenses."

"It was a promise," he said, "and here's what I want. Go out with me tonight."

"Go out with you? Like a date? I can't do that."

"No date. We'll call it a business meeting." He nodded. "That's right, an official partnership meeting."

Gwen had an uneasy conviction that sharing an evening with Robert would have nothing whatsoever to do with business. "Robert, you know I can't go out with you."

"Your boyfriend's not here to squire you around like he should. But I am."

The worst of it was that she *wanted* to be with Robert tonight. Even after all the aggravation, all the turmoil, she wanted to be with the man who threatened her restaurant. Gwen held her arms more tightly against her body.

"It doesn't matter that Scott's not here," she said. "As long as I'm wearing his ring, I'm not going to spend an evening with you or any other man."

It was dark now. The lantern light glimmered, fickle as a firefly, and Gwen couldn't read the expression on Robert's face. He set the lantern on the porch railing.

"You're wasting your time on that guy—he doesn't deserve your loyalty. But remember, Gwennie, you still owe me. Eventually I'm going to collect."

Then Robert went down the steps and disappeared into the night, leaving Gwen with all her unspoken longings. Leaving her alone.

GWEN NUDGED the wretched plastic sheeting that still separated her side of the restaurant from Robert's. This morning was the official unveiling, and she wanted to get on with it. It was time for Plan C to go into action! Gwen nudged the plastic again. Now she saw a shadowy figure moving behind it, a tall broad-shouldered figure that looked domineering even when hazy like this.

"Impatient, Gwennie?" Robert asked from the other side of the barrier. "You keep telling me I should learn how to relax and enjoy the moment. Here's a moment to enjoy."

"Maybe you're afraid to let me see what you did over there. Maybe it's a disaster area."

"All right, here goes. You're going to like it, Gwennie. Stand back...." He ripped down the plastic sheeting with a flourish, and Gwen's curiosity of the last few days was finally satisfied.

Well, maybe "satisfied" wasn't the right word. "Chagrin" was a more appropriate term for what she experienced as she first glanced around. Reluctantly she had to admit that Robert and his contractors had done an excellent job of remodeling; the place was much lighter and more airy than before. The walls had been painted a pleasing shade of apricot, with a wainscoting of light pine. A few Monet prints hung here and there, water scenes in shimmering blues.

Robert had made other changes, too. Gwen walked slowly through his side of the restaurant, noting all the details. He'd gotten rid of the big rough-hewn tables that had been there before, replacing them with much smaller ones in a wood that matched the pine of the wainscoting.

"Very clever," Gwen murmured. "You've managed to pack a whole lot more tables in here without making the place look crammed. Light colors everywhere—that helps...."

"Knew you'd like it."

Gwen frowned. "I'm not saying I like it. Sure, I'll admit that what you've done is effective. But it seems to me you want to stuff people in like so many anchovies on a pizza, hoping they won't realize they'll need a shoehorn to scratch their noses."

Robert didn't appear disturbed by her comments. "Over here, Gwennie. Look at this." He gestured proudly at a snazzy new buffet table, also built of light pine. Gwen walked around it, observing it critically from every angle. Silver warming pans of all shapes and sizes were fitted neatly in the top of the table. Shining metal, polished wood—yes, the buffet was very impressive.

"State-of-the-art," Robert said, opening a door below the table and pointing out several complicated oven controls. "This baby'll keep each dish at the perfect temperature. I'll have every kind of pasta out here and every kind of sauce. Quick, easy, convenient for the customer. You take your linguine, ladle on some clam sauce, chow down—and you're outta here."

Gwen walked around the buffet table one more time, giving all its modern gadgetry a contemptuous glare. "I see. Your idea is to create a sort of fast-food Italian restaurant. Slap on the spaghetti so you can move more customers through."

Robert nodded. "You've got the picture, Gwennie. Of course, I'll still be serving up eggplant parmigiana and cannoli for people who want them. It's a great combination. Quick food with a little atmosphere thrown in—that's what restaurant customers really want."

"Not *my* customers," Gwen declared. "They want to linger over a good home-style meal, not feel like someone can't wait to push them out the door!"

"So let's see what you did on your side, Gwendolyn. Should be interesting."

Gwen was more than happy to lead the way across to her turf. She'd left the walls the same ivory-tinged plaster as before, but she'd taken down the dark heavy tapestries that had once obscured this part of the room. In their place she'd hung colorful posters of Italy—Lake Como, the canals of Venice, a view of the Adriatic. It struck Gwen that, like Robert, she'd chosen water scenes to decorate her side. But all similarity ended there. Gwen had kept the big rustic tables that allowed her customers plenty of elbow room. She'd brightened them with new tablecloths and napkins in cornflower blue, the Christmas centerpieces providing more bright color.

"Get a look at this," Gwen told Robert, ushering him over to one of the front windows. Here she'd placed the crowning detail of her decorating scheme:

an antique bicycle with wide fenders painted the same cornflower blue as her tablecloths. She'd filled the straw basket between the handlebars with a Christmas bouquet of holly sprigs and evergreen boughs. The bicycle, framed by the window, was like a whimsical painting. Gwen knew it was the perfect touch, and she gestured at it as proudly as Robert had pointed out his new-fangled buffet table.

"Now, *this* is atmosphere," she said. "My customers will be able to sit back, see the sun shining through the window on those bicycle fenders—and imagine they're pedaling off to all sorts of wonderful destinations. And they won't have to dish up their own lasagna."

Robert made no comment. He surveyed the bicycle with slightly raised eyebrows, then wandered around the rest of Gwen's side. He perused each poster of Italy and stopped beside a small alcove that had once harbored a rather alarming rubber plant. Gwen had donated the rubber plant to Claudine, and in its place she had put a glass-fronted bookshelf. Robert bent down to scan the books she'd placed carefully on the shelves. When he was finished with that, he straightened up to examine the prints Gwen had hung above: ink sketches of Venetian villas and Roman statues and crowded Neapolitan streets, drawn more than a century ago by a young American artist who had wandered throughout Italy. Robert considered all this, yet still said nothing. Gwen twitched a corner on one of her new tablecloths.

''Well, what do you think?'' she demanded at last. It irked her no end that Robert's opinion was suddenly so important to her.

He rubbed his jaw thoughtfully. ''If I could use only one word to describe what your side is like, the word is 'romantic.' Yep, this place reeks of romance.''

She glanced around in consternation. ''That's not true. It's warm, friendly—homey, even. But definitely not romantic! That wasn't my intention at all.''

''Gwennie, open your eyes. First off, you've got all these idyllic posters of Italy on the walls. You've got those books about Italian gardens, and ones by Victorian poets jaunting off to Italy. And we haven't even discussed that wobbly old bike yet. Lord, it's the bicycle of a mush-heart. Nobody else would see any potential in it.''

''It's part of a decorating scheme, that's all,'' Gwen protested. ''I never thought of actually riding it.'' She hated that amused look on Robert's face—and she hated realizing that she *had* thought about riding that quaint old bike. She'd pictured herself pedaling it past sunny Italian gardens and olive groves, the ribbons of her straw hat fluttering behind her in the breeze, and beside her some dashing man pedaling away on his own bike, a man with dark curling hair and an infuriating smile....

I don't believe myself! Gwen thought in disgust. Where did she get these absurd delusions, anyway? If Robert Beltramo ever *did* end up cruising on a bicycle beside her, he'd be leaning over the handlebars of a flashy twelve-speed, chuckling as he left her behind in the dust.

"I'll tell you what this place really looks like," Robert said now. "It looks like some kind of wistful Victorian travel agency for people who want to go to Italy but probably will never get there."

Gwen crammed her hands into the pockets of the apron she'd bought especially for the reopening of the restaurant. "Wistful travel agency—you're wrong about that, Beltramo. My side of the restaurant is a place for people who *do* things, not just for people who dream. If a person dreams of going to Italy, if a person longs for the gondolas of Venice and the cathedrals of Rome, well, maybe my posters and books and even my bicycle will inspire that person to grab the next flight across the Atlantic!"

"Gwennie, I can call the airport and book you a flight today. I hate to see you stifling your dreams. Maybe the airline would even let you take your old rattletrap of a bike along."

Gwen clenched her hands inside her pockets. "I'm not stifling myself, dammit. I *will* go to Italy—someday."

"You'll tow old Scott along, instead of the bike, that it?"

"No, that's *not* it. Scott doesn't like the sound of Italy—too many buildings leaning one way or another, he says. I'll go on my own."

Robert brought out his obnoxious notepad and his father's leaky fountain pen. He started jotting notes again. "This is good," he said, as if to himself. "This is real good."

"Beltramo, what are you doing?"

"Expanding the con list on your boyfriend. Somebody's got to do it. Con number twelve: old Scott refuses to go to Italy. Take my advice, Gwennie. Never marry a guy who refuses to go to Italy."

She craned her neck, trying to see what he was writing. "You can't possibly have thought up twelve reasons I shouldn't marry Scott."

"Try me, Gwennie. Ask me what reason number six is."

"This is ridiculous."

"Go ahead, ask."

"Okay." She sighed. "What is reason number six?"

He scanned his pad with great concentration. "Number six...here we go. Reason number six you shouldn't marry this guy—he likes your cooking."

"That's a pro, Beltramo, remember? That definitely belongs on the pro side." Gwen strode to the sideboard where she kept extra supplies and began folding more cornflower-blue napkins.

Robert came over to watch what she was doing. "Gwennie, you marry a guy who likes your cooking, and what do you have? Somebody who expects you to put a hot dinner on the table every night. This isn't a person who'll take you out to eat. He figures you can cook better than anyone else, so why bother? Furthermore—"

"No furthermore." Gwen had almost tied one of the napkins in knots. "What do you suggest I do? Hook up with some guy who tells me I don't know how to make tortellini or my minestrone doesn't have enough garlic?"

"You can't cook real Italian if you're afraid of garlic, that's what I always say."

"I *know* it's what you always say." Gwen wadded up a napkin. Robert was standing close to her, and she could hardly think straight anymore. She took a deep breath, and at least one thing seemed clear to her. She turned and gazed at Robert.

"I have to tell Scott," she said. "I have to tell him exactly what's been going on around here."

Robert looked interested. "What do you mean, Gwennie? What exactly will you tell him?"

"Everything." She focused on the flannel cloth of Robert's shirt. It was gray flannel, the color of a soft winter fog that could wrap itself right around you. "I'll tell him that you kissed me on the porch swing, and—"

"Don't forget about the time I kissed you under the mistletoe," Robert murmured.

Gwen stuffed her hands into her pockets again, anything to avoid reaching out to touch the soft flannel. "I'll tell Scott everything," she repeated. "As soon as he gets back in town, that's what I'll do. If he and I discuss the situation, get it all out in the open, I'm sure we can resolve it. I've been trying to resolve things on my own, and that's a mistake."

Robert hooked a thumb in one of his belt loops. He wore a big silver belt buckle shaped like an ornery Texas bull about to charge. That seemed entirely appropriate for the bullheaded Robert Beltramo.

"What else will you tell Scott?" he asked. "Maybe you should tell him you're going off to Italy on your own because he doesn't give you enough romance. Or maybe you should tell him he doesn't have the right fit for your porch swing...."

Gwen turned back to the sideboard and wadded up another napkin. "I'll tell him that, because of you, my restaurant has turned into some bizarre combination of a fast-food joint and a travel agency. You know what else? I'll tell him you like to drive me bonkers because it keeps you from facing your own problems. It keeps you from facing whatever *really* brought you back to San Antonio. And I'll tell him...I'll tell him that maybe you kissed me, but it didn't mean anything to you!"

"You really believe all that?" he asked.

"Yes...yes, I do. I'm convinced you're using me, Robert. You're using me and the restaurant to avoid something in your own life. Something that has to do with your father—that's what I'm still willing to bet."

Robert's expression gave nothing away. "And when I kissed you, Gwennie, you honestly believe it didn't mean anything to me?"

"I suppose you found those kisses pleasant enough. But they're just part of your railroading your way into my life. You want to take my restaurant, and you want to take a few kisses along the way, too, and afterward you'll barrel off to some new goal." She stared at Robert defiantly. "You're not going to get the restaurant, Beltramo. I'm going to give you one humdinger of a battle. And no more kisses! You got it? No more kisses."

"No more," he repeated solemnly. Then he cupped her face with both hands, smiled at her and planted a firm no-nonsense kiss on her mouth. He stepped back. "We'll have none of that, Gwennie."

Then he whistled all the way into the kitchen.

CHAPTER EIGHT

A FEW DAYS LATER, Gwen felt like a frantic juggler with twenty different balls in the air. Any minute now one of those balls could go crashing to the ground...but she couldn't allow herself even to think about that. She *had* to keep everything moving. Rather wildly she pushed a casserole dish of manicotti into the oven, stirred the bolognese sauce on the grill and started heating a pot of water for another batch of fettuccine. Her apron was spattered even more than usual, the dairyman was late with the extra delivery of cheese, her mushroom pies still weren't finished—and Robert Beltramo was watching everything she did from his own side of the kitchen.

"Lord," he grumbled. "Working in the same room with you is like jumping into a vat of hot soup. Everything's boiling over into chaos." Efficiently, methodically, Robert shaped a meatball in both hands and tossed it into a frying pan with a whole bunch of other orderly meatballs.

"You know," Gwen said, vigorously cranking open a can of tuna, "I wish you'd learn how to cook with a little creative chaos yourself. It really gets on my nerves, the way you're so darn organized. No chef can get inspired without at least a little mess."

"Inspiration," he said over his pan of meatballs. "I'll tell you what I'm inspired to do. I'd like to fire-hose the spaghetti sauce off the ceiling and start fresh."

"You won't have a chance. Come Christmas Eve, you're out of here." Gwen darted to the stove, pulled a tray of roasted peppers from the broiler and promptly burned her hand. "Damn! I don't have time for this. The lunch rush is going to start any minute!"

Robert came over before she could protest and led her to the sink. Holding her hand, he ran cool water over the burn.

"You're trying to do too much, Gwennie. Catering meals on riverboats, opening the restaurant before the sun's even up to serve breakfast—what'll you do next?"

"Whatever it takes to beat you." For some reason she let him go on holding her hand under the tap. The cool water felt good, plus she needed a few minutes to catch her breath—and Robert's touch felt good, too, darn it. But when she did try to pull away, he wouldn't let her.

"You have to take care of this burn. And you should relax a little. Where's all this scramble getting you? Look at how it's gone—I counter your every move. You cater dinner on one of the riverboats—I cater lunch the next day. You start serving break-fast—I start serving breakfast, too."

"Right," Gwen muttered. "Italian omelets to go, crammed into those little cardboard boxes of yours."

"People sure seem to like 'em, don't they? Carry-out omelets. Don't know how I came up with such a good idea."

She wiggled her fingers in his grasp. "You came up with it by snooping over here on my side, watching *me* make zucchini omelets. At least I have the decency to serve them on china plates. Listen, Beltramo, I don't have time to lounge around like this."

"You have to relax, or you're liable to end up hurting yourself all over again. Let's see what shape your hand's in." He turned off the faucet and examined the burn critically. "Hmm. Not too bad."

His fingers were gentle and warm on hers. Gwen stood there beside him at the sink, thinking how ironic it was that now Robert Beltramo was counseling *her* to relax. Fact of the matter was, she'd been plenty relaxed before he'd barged into her life. He was the reason everything seemed to have turned upside down. But she went on standing there with him, torn between worry over her mushroom pies and a need simply to be with Robert like this—not competing, not battling each other, but merely allowing the winter sunshine to spill onto them through the windowpane, the pungent aroma of the dried herbs on the sill wafting over them. But this need frightened Gwen. Did she really want to be near the man who threatened the restaurant she loved? Did she really want to be near the man who wasn't her fiancé? All the while her emotions swirled into deeper and deeper confusion, and every minute Christmas Eve loomed closer and closer.

Robert nudged the big diamond sparkling on her finger. "Some behemoth, Gwennie. Scares me every time I look at it."

She snatched her hand away. "Scott and I are working things out, you know. Last night we got everything into the open."

"He's actually in town? In person?"

"He left again this morning," Gwen said defensively. "But the two of us had a frank and constructive discussion over dinner."

"You cooked, didn't you, Gwennie?"

She went to uncover her pastry dough. "Of course I cooked. I like cooking for someone who enjoys my food." Gwen didn't want to admit that since her engagement, Scott hadn't taken her out to a single restaurant. No way would she admit that to Robert. "Anyhow, when I told Scott about you and our little kissing incident under the mistletoe, he was very understanding—the Christmas spirit and all. But when I told him about the other incidents, the ones on the porch and in the restaurant, well, of course he was concerned. Very concerned."

Robert grinned slowly. "What did he say, Gwennie?"

She glared at Robert. "Dammit, he said, 'please pass the pastrami'!"

"You know what I'm going to tell you, Gwendolyn. Never trust a guy who can eat pastrami even when he knows you kissed somebody else on the porch swing."

Gwen thumped her pastry dough. "I'm lucky to be engaged to a man who doesn't fly off the handle just because . . . well, just because another man got carried away on the porch swing! And under the mistletoe and . . .'' She was getting off track. "Scott is a wonderful person," she went on briskly. "A man who's willing to work through a problem, instead of getting all jealous and bent out of shape, is someone special, that's all."

"If your boyfriend's this amenable, you ought to bring him in and introduce him to me. Maybe we'll all be friends."

"Scott isn't *that* reasonable, for goodness' sake." Gwen feared, however, that Scott might very well be that reasonable. Last night she'd truly admired her fiancé's sensible behavior. But now Gwen wished he hadn't been quite so understanding. If only he were a little more ardent about things. . . .

Robert leaned companionably against the counter. "Watch out, or you're going to pummel that dough into oblivion. Gwennie, maybe if I kiss you again, that'll keep your boyfriend home for good. Maybe it's all in a good cause, my kissing you."

Gwen flushed and tried very hard not to conjure up the memory of Robert's lips on hers. "Beltramo, don't you have some spaghetti you need to stuff into little cardboard boxes or something?"

"Everything's under control on my side, Gwendolyn. Everything."

She stared at him in exasperation. Yes, he seemed quite under control. Those kisses hadn't thrown *him* into a tailspin, whereas Gwen was on the verge of ruining her wise, sensible engagement—all because of a man who could kiss her so effectively and then joke about it as if it had meant nothing at all.

"I'm really going to do it," she declared suddenly, giving the pastry dough one more punch. "Come Christmas Eve, I'm finally going to set the wedding date!"

Robert straightened up from the counter. An unreadable expression flashed across his face. "Scott's going to be in town Christmas Eve, Gwennie?"

"Of course he is. And I *am* going to set the date."

"If it makes you feel safe," Robert said quietly.

"I don't want to be safe. I want...I just want..." She couldn't finish the sentence. All she could do was stare across the counter at Robert, trying to battle some silent unnameable challenge in his eyes. A mysterious, stormy challenge that had nothing to do with fiancés or restaurants, only Gwen and Robert....

Claudine burst into the kitchen, red hair flying. "Gwen!" she squeaked in agitation. "Come here— quick!"

Somehow Gwen still couldn't tear her gaze away from Robert. His eyes were very dark, yet shimmering with their own special light, the color of deep topaz.

"Claudine...isn't it something you can take care of yourself?" she asked distractedly.

"No. No, it's not!" Claudine seemed particularly flustered. She grabbed hold of Gwen's arm and propelled her through the swinging door to the dining area. Then, excitedly, words began tumbling helterskelter from Claudine's mouth. "She's here, Gwen! She's here. She's that one sitting over there by the window, all by herself, with all that long gorgeous blond hair. Don't you just hate women with hair like that? I didn't know who she was at first—I mean, how was I supposed to know? But then she told me who she was, in this snooty voice like I'm supposed to be all overawed and maybe curtsy or something, if you can believe it."

"Slow down," Gwen said. "Are you saying that woman is actually—"

"Leda Thatcher," Claudine whispered urgently. "You got her here, Gwen! I can't believe you did it, but she's right here in Pop's Restaurant."

Now Gwen was in danger of becoming as flustered as Claudine. Leda Thatcher was San Antonio's number-one food critic. If she gave Gwen's menu a good review in her newspaper, well, people would be lining up clear down the River Walk to eat on Gwen's side of the restaurant. These past few days, she hadn't dared to hope she'd succeed in luring the food critic here to sample her cooking. But she'd done it—she'd actually done it. And *this* time Robert Beltramo wasn't going to interfere.

Gwen quickly untied her splattered apron, wadded it up and stuffed it onto one of the bus trays. "Okay, Claudine, this is what I want you to do. Keep Robert occupied. Talk to him. Distract him. Spill tomato sauce on him, if that's what it takes. Anything. Do not, under any circumstances, let that man out of the kitchen!"

"Don't worry, I'll take care of it. This is so-o-o neat. I mean, this time we've really done it. What a coup!"

"Hurry, before Robert gets suspicious." Gwen steered Claudine back toward the kitchen, then advanced on Leda Thatcher's table.

"Ms. Thatcher, I'm Gwen Ferris. I'm so pleased you could accept my invitation."

Leda Thatcher surveyed Gwen coolly. The woman was pretty, although she had an oddly narrow face. Her features were narrow, too, delicate and precise as if they had been drawn in with a fine-line pencil. She was younger than Gwen had expected, surely no older than thirty or so. But her manner was that of a duchess condescending to address the downstairs maid.

"Ms. Ferris, I hope you realize I have a very busy schedule. This little impromptu visit isn't the type of thing I'm accustomed to doing. I only came here today because your persistence intrigued me." Leda delicately nibbled a flaky morsel of white fish with rosemary. And then, just as delicately, she swirled angel-hair pasta around her fork.

"Perhaps you'd like some more of the bread salad," Gwen suggested. "Or more soup."

"This will do. I must admit your truffle soup is actually tolerable."

Maybe Gwen was mistaken, but it seemed Leda had just complimented the truffle soup. Unfortunately Leda also appeared to have a curious nature. She glanced over toward Robert's side.

"How frightfully original," Leda murmured. "The signs outside indicate that you have divided this establishment down the middle. Your Italian cuisine on one side, Robert Beltramo's Italian eatery on the other. And who, pray tell, is Robert Beltramo?"

Gwen shifted position in an effort to block the view of Robert's area. "It's a very long story, Ms. Thatcher. Let's just say that *my* side truly represents the spirit of Pop's Restaurant—"

"And my side represents the spirit of a good quick meal" came Robert's voice, directly behind Gwen. She whirled around in dismay, just in time to see him give Leda Thatcher his engaging grin. Then he spoke to Leda with his hint of a Texas drawl. "Ms. Thatcher, it so happens I'm Robert Beltramo. And I'd like to invite you over for the best damn Italian food you've ever tasted. Are you ready?"

Leda Thatcher didn't answer Robert's question at first, but merely pursed her delicate lips with an air of speculation. Claudine hovered in the background, looking intensely apologetic. Gwen scowled intensely at Robert. And Robert gave another of his infuriatingly attractive smiles. That smile seemed directed solely at Leda Thatcher, a fact that irked Gwen more than anything. But she knew she couldn't let Robert ruin this moment for her. She just couldn't!

"Ms. Thatcher, I've prepared a dessert I'm sure you'll want to sample," Gwen said firmly. "Chestnut pudding with whipped cream and just a touch of chocolate—"

"*Sebadas,*" Robert murmured, Italy mingling with the Texas in his voice. "That's what you'll find over there in my neck of the woods, Ms. Thatcher. If you've never tasted one of 'em, you don't know what you're missing. We're talking about a turnover with a twist, deep fried until the cheese melts inside, and then you douse the whole thing with honey while it's still sizzling.''

"Pistachio ice cream, Ms. Thatcher," Gwen said in her most persuasive voice. "Pistachio ice cream made fresh with ricotta cheese and molded with slices of candied pear."

"Zabaglione," Robert countered, a dangerous glint in his eye. Now he was looking straight at Gwen. "Custard rich as you can get it with Marsala wine and heaped with strawberries."

"My, my," Leda murmured. "This culinary duel is most entertaining. Perhaps I had better see what it's all about. Mr. Beltramo, *do* give me a tour of your side."

"Ms. Thatcher," Gwen said rather desperately. "The chestnut pudding—"

Leda waved her delicate fingers, as if to dismiss Gwen's pudding without another thought. "I like the idea of reviewing a restaurant in competition with itself. In order to do so, I must know all about this singular arrangement." She rose gracefully and tucked her hand into the crook of Robert's arm. "Do tell me, Mr. Beltramo, how did this division occur?"

Robert began gallantly escorting Leda Thatcher over to his side, although he craned his head back in Gwen's direction and gave her a wink. "Ms. Thatcher, let's just say Gwennie and I came up with a novel publicity scheme to advertise Pop's Restaurant. And it's taken off with itself. It's a big success."

Gwen clenched her hands as the two of them strolled away. She couldn't believe Robert had winked at her. And stolen her food critic, to boot!

Claudine hurried over to Gwen. "O-o-h, I'm sorry," she said breathlessly. "I just couldn't keep him in the kitchen. You know how he is. I mean, somehow he knew something was up. It's like he has a nose for these things. What are we going to do now?"

"You're going to stay here and man the fort," Gwen instructed. "And I'm going to make sure Robert Beltramo doesn't get away with this." She strode after Robert and Leda, catching up to them just as Robert was beginning a tour of his fancy buffet table. He glanced over at Gwen.

"Looks like you have some more customers trooping in. Don't let us keep you tied up."

"Claudine can handle the place for a while. I wouldn't miss this for anything." Gwen stayed right at Robert's elbow. "Don't forget to tell Ms. Thatcher how each warming pan is individually monitored and controlled by a sensitive thermostatic device. That way you can provide your customers with a whole variety of pasta-to-go."

"Italian fast food," Robert said imperturbably. "Ms. Thatcher, that's what I offer—fettuccine on the fly. No wait, no worry. Eat your rigatoni and run."

He had no shame, he really didn't. Next thing you knew, he'd be whipping out those little cardboard boxes of his and demonstrating how he packed omelets into them. Fine. Surely nothing could offend Leda Thatcher's refined sensibilities more than Robert's "chow down" philosophy for his customers. Gwen smiled in grim satisfaction at the thought, only to hear Leda begin rhapsodizing about Robert Beltramo's fast-food Italian eatery.

"What a truly marvelous idea. Hurry-up cuisine, instead of haute cuisine. A true entrepreneur is wise to realize the advantages of such an approach. And do call me Leda...Roberto." Leda took a plate from one end of the buffet table and in her delicate precise manner began dishing up tagliatelle pasta with diced bacon. Meanwhile, "Roberto" looked all too pleased with himself. Gwen curled her fingers in her palms. An odd uncomfortable emotion she couldn't identify churned inside her. She tried to ignore it as she watched Leda take a sampling of marinara sauce from one of Robert's obnoxious silver warming pans. Then Leda sailed over to one of Robert's obnoxious little tables and sat down. Robert sat across from Leda. And Gwen pulled up a chair and plunked herself down right between the two of them.

Robert nodded over toward her side of the restaurant. "Claudine looks a little frazzled, handling all those customers on her own."

"I think she's doing an excellent job," Gwen declared, although Claudine did, indeed, look frazzled as she balanced four loaded lunch plates in her arms. "What about your own customers, Roberto? Poor Jeremy's being run off his feet."

"Hey, I've trained him well. He doesn't slouch around the way he used to." Robert leaned back in his chair, relaxed yet still retaining an aura of command. Leda surveyed him as if he were dessert and she couldn't wait to start nibbling. And Robert didn't seem to mind at all being perused by a pretty female as if he were a piece of chocolate torte. After a minute he raised his hand to signal Jeremy. Robert murmured a few low instructions, and Jeremy dashed toward the kitchen. Moments later he dashed back out again bearing a tray of delicacies that he arranged in front of Leda: golden fried *sebadas* complete with a dish of honey, cannoli rolled with a creamy filling of ricotta and dusted in powdered sugar, wedges of fruit pie. To Gwen's chagrin, her mouth started watering. She'd barely eaten three bites at breakfast and hadn't even been able to think about lunch yet. Why did Robert's cannoli have to look so enticing?

"As long as you're here, might as well have something to eat, Gwennie," he said, as if hunger was written all over her face. "Go ahead—dig in." That ever present humor glimmered in his eyes.

"No, thank you," she said stiffly, hoping her stomach wouldn't start rumbling in protest.

She turned toward Leda. "Ms. Thatcher, wouldn't you be more comfortable back on my side of the restaurant? You'd actually have enough room to spread your elbows."

Leda patted her lips with one of Robert's paper napkins. "Dear me," she murmured. "If I remain caught in the middle of you two, I will simply be forced to eat my way into oblivion. I'm afraid I must turn you down, Ms. Ferris, but you *have* given me an excellent idea. In order for me to do justice to Roberto's food, I believe he will have to cook dinner for me. At my house tonight would be a most convenient time. Say, ten-ish?" Leda gazed expectantly across the table at Robert. He rubbed his jaw thoughtfully, as if actually considering the idea. And Gwen sat between the two of them, stewing for all she was worth. She wondered how in tarnation she had managed to inspire such a cockeyed scheme in Leda Thatcher's head! Robert Beltramo, cooking an intimate meal for Leda and then serving that meal to her, perhaps by candlelight...

Gwen made a sound that came out somewhere between a squawk and a moan. Both Leda and Robert looked at her inquiringly, but she couldn't say a thing. That strange emotion swirled inside her again, and this time she recognized it. Jealousy. That was it—pure, unadulterated, unmitigated jealousy, a sensation that Scott had never once induced in her. A sensation so unpleasant and so distressing that all Gwen could do was sit there frozen between Leda Thatcher and Roberto Beltramo.

"I don't know why it can't be arranged," he remarked. "Dinner tonight at your house, Leda."

"Wonderful. I'll be looking forward to it. I do so like a man who knows how to cook. Don't you, Ms. Ferris? But I must be off. Goodbye for now, Roberto. Remember, ten-ish. I live in the King William district—call my secretary and she'll tell you how to get to my house." Leda Thatcher sailed regally out of the restaurant, an energetic Jeremy sprinting to open the door for her.

Robert had risen from his chair at Leda's departure, but now he sat down again. He studied Gwen solemnly. "You look kind of funny. Maybe it's lack of food. Chefs feed everybody else, but never themselves. Here, have some of this." He set a piece of fruit pie in front of her, but Gwen's appetite had vanished.

She hated being jealous. She downright detested the feeling!

Gwen spread both hands flat on the table. "How did you find out Leda was coming to my side of the restaurant? If you'd just stayed in the kitchen today, darn it..."

"Couldn't do that, Gwennie. Not after the way you've been locking yourself in the office the past couple of days to make all those mysterious phone calls. Yesterday I had Jeremy discreetly pump Claudine for information. That part was easy—the guy's a pro. Claudine spilled the beans without even knowing she was spilling them. I tell you, Jeremy's got potential."

"I can't believe you'd be so devious," Gwen muttered. "You and Jeremy both."

"No more devious than you, Gwendolyn. You were going to sneak a food critic in here without letting me in on the fun. I'm pretty disappointed at that sort of underhand behavior coming from you."

"There was nothing underhand about it. I used my own ingenuity to get Leda Thatcher here, and then you sabotaged me. But why am I bothering to argue with you? It never does me any good!" Gwen drummed her fingers on the table, making the plates clatter in a rhythm of frustration. "So you're really going to do it. You're going to cook dinner for her."

Robert picked up a *sebada* and started munching on it himself. "Really bothers you, doesn't it, my cooking dinner for Leda. Can't think why, your being engaged and all. Thought you'd be happy to see me getting out and socializing a little."

The whole situation was going from bad to worse. Not only was Gwen prickling with jealousy, she was allowing it to show. She slapped her hand down on the table so forcefully that people at other tables looked over in curiosity. Gwen stood up.

"R.B.," she said in a low voice, "you can socialize with twenty gorgeous females, for all I care. But next time find your own food critic, okay?"

Robert took another crunchy bite of *sebada*. "Does this mean you and your fiancé will want to double-date with Leda and me?"

"When pancakes sing," she said dryly.

Robert gazed at her with just a ghost of a smile. Gwen would have enjoyed pouring the dish of honey over his head, but she controlled herself. All she did was grab one of his *sebadas* before striding back to her side of the restaurant where she belonged. She bit into the *sebada,* quite annoyed when the morsel tasted as good as it looked. Every bit as good.

CHAPTER NINE

THE LIGHT from the kitchen windows streamed out over the small basketball court behind Pop's Restaurant. Robert dribbled the ball, then leapt up to take a shot. The ball went through the hoop, clean and swift. Robert pounded down the court again, his body capturing the joy of motion even in the shadows of night.

Gwen stood in the back doorway, watching Robert and at the same time detesting herself for lingering here. But all day she'd been tormented by her vivid imagination—picturing how Leda and Robert would be together tonight. Even more tormenting was the thought that she *shouldn't* be tormented. It shouldn't matter to her at all how Robert spent his time with a beautiful women. In fact, it should make her grateful she was engaged to Scott, a man too wrapped up in computer programs to care about romancing other women. Too wrapped up in computer programs to care about romancing *her,* for that matter—but nothing was perfect in life. Gwen knew she ought to be grateful, that was all.

Somehow none of this cheered her in the least. She was wound up tight inside. She'd never felt like this before. She was used to being relaxed and happy, at ease with herself. Robert Beltramo had changed all that. She looked on as he shot the ball again, and then she stepped onto the court.

"It's almost ten," she said. "You're going to be late."

Robert bounced the ball from one hand to the other. "Don't worry. Leda will get her dinner tonight, cooked personally by me."

"I'm not worried. But if you're going to do it, just do it. Go and leave me in peace."

Now Robert stopped dribbling the ball, balancing it, instead, on his fingers. "You're the one who came looking for me tonight, Gwennie. I cleared out of the kitchen a while ago. I left you in peace."

Gwen wandered restlessly over the court. "It doesn't matter. I knew you were out here with that ball, shooting baskets over and over. That's enough to distract anybody."

"I'm just retracing old steps," he said slowly. "When I was a kid, I used to come out here and practice for hours, late into the night. It meant I could delay going home as long as I wanted...."

Gwen sensed a tension in Robert that seemed an echo of her own. She went to lean against the wooden post that supported the basketball hoop, stuffing her hands into the pockets of her jeans.

"Was it that bad going home to your father? I can't believe that it really was."

"Hell, yes, it was bad." Robert gave the ball one bounce against the concrete. "When the old guy wasn't yelling, he'd slump in a chair and just stare at the television screen. The silence—I hated that almost more than the yelling."

"Maybe he was lonely. Because that's how I saw him. A lonely old man who didn't know how to reach out to people, but who wanted to reach out more than anything. He was like Scrooge—he had a good heart buried underneath all the meanness."

Robert came closer, gazing at her in the dim light. "It's always the underdog with you, isn't it, Gwennie?"

"It's not that simple. I honestly cared about your father. Somebody had to care. You went off, Robert. You left him here alone without a family."

"I had to leave," Robert said in a harsh voice. "My father wanted me to be like him, to turn as miserable and mean as he was. But I knew I could never be like that. I did everything I could to get away—even applied for a basketball scholarship at a college out of state. When I didn't get that scholarship, my father almost seemed happy for the first time in years. Genuinely happy. I guess he thought it'd make me stay at the restaurant forever, complaining about the bad turn life had given me. He never figured I'd just find another way to make it to college."

Gwen couldn't help admiring Robert. He possessed a vibrancy and a determination that his father had never had.

"Maybe Pop was just afraid that if you went off to college, he'd lose you. And he didn't know how to tell you that."

Robert frowned down at the ball in his hands. "Believe it or not, I thought about that, too. I tried to understand the old guy. He was my father, after all. That's why I came back to San Antonio the summer after I graduated from college. I wanted to patch things up. But—'' He stopped abruptly, swearing under his breath. "Ferris, you did it again. You're like some bartender people can't help confiding in. Your customers, me—everybody. Probably even strangers on the street stop to tell you their problems. It's one hell of a nuisance. You've made me start talking about something that's over and done with.''

"You need to talk, only you're too stubborn to admit it. That's at least one thing you and Pop had in common—sheer mule-headedness.''

All the frustration and restlessness in Gwen threatened to boil over. The next thing she did was purely an impulse. She snatched the ball out of Robert's hands, dribbled it up and down the court and then hurtled it full force toward the hoop. She missed, the ball thumping against the backboard, but she caught it again. She stood in the middle of the court, holding the ball and taking a deep gulp of air. She felt a release from some of her tension. If she pounded up and down the court, giving herself over to sheer physical movement, maybe she could forget about all her problems with the restaurant and Scott—and even her problems with Robert....

He took the ball from her before she could even think about defending herself, and he charged toward the hoop. Still without thought, with only a need for motion, Gwen raced after him. She tried to block his way, but he soared up easily and made his shot. Another basket. Gwen captured the ball and dodged him, but she wasn't very adept and Robert quickly gained the ball again.

Back and forth they went, fighting for the ball. Robert gave her no allowances for inexperience or lack of skill, but she didn't want any. This seemed just one more way to battle him, one more way to struggle against the assault he'd made on her mind and heart. If she focused on the ball, only on the ball, somehow she'd win. . . .

Neither one of them spoke, and it became a silent contest of wills. Robert feinted a move to the left, then headed right, his shoulder brushing Gwen's. Next she bumped full against him as she tried to wrest the ball away. This elemental physical contact with Robert was something unfamiliar to her, as if she were learning the steps of a new dance, a rough-and-tumble dance that both disturbed and enticed her. Sweat dampened her skin in the cool humid air and her breath came unevenly. In a brief second of opportunity she aimed the ball toward the basket, sending it through the net. She swiveled exultantly toward Robert.

"There! I did it. I finally got the darn ball through the hoop!"

Robert laughed softly in the night. "You've proved me right, Gwennie. I knew you'd be good on a basketball court. Damn good." He looked more attractive than ever as he spoke, his dark hair tumbling over his forehead from the exertion of the game. Gwen rubbed her arms, and suddenly this game of theirs seemed much too intimate. It hadn't helped banish any of her confusion, after all. It had only aggravated the complicated longings she didn't even know how to name. She and Robert stared at each other, and she knew there was no simple way to solve what was between them, no simple way at all.

"Aren't you going to Leda's?" Gwen asked, hearing the brittleness in her voice.

"Do you want me to go?"

She wouldn't answer that question. She was afraid of what her answer might be. "Just go," she said. "Please."

Robert waited another moment, studying her. She refused to betray any emotion to him, keeping her face stiff. And then he did turn and leave her. He left her with all the yearning and jealousy she had no right to feel—the yearning and jealousy that could break her heart if somehow she didn't protect herself in time.

LATE THE NEXT AFTERNOON, Leda Thatcher floated into the kitchen of Pop's Restaurant. That was right—she floated. Gwen stopped working the pasta machine and stared at her. Goodness, the woman's face glowed. It almost seemed as if her narrow features had softened and filled out a little. She stopped on the other side of the counter and smiled beneficently at Gwen.

"Hello, Gwennie, hello. Is Roberto here?" Even her voice sounded fuller and warmer than yesterday.

Gwen cringed at the use of her nickname. "Robert's in the office, meeting with one of his suppliers. Excuse me, but is that a basketball jersey you're wearing?"

Leda twirled around, exhibiting her bright red jersey, complemented nicely by white jeans. "It doesn't have my name yet, of course, but I couldn't wait to wear it. Isn't it wonderful? I've decided to be number twenty-four.''

Gwen gave the handle of the pasta machine a good hard crank. ''Ms. Thatcher, I'm almost afraid to ask. Is it possible...is it possible you're actually going to join...'' Gwen couldn't get the words out, but Leda had no trouble finishing for her.

''I'm the newest member of the Beltramo Buccaneers,'' she said airily, tossing back her mane of blond hair. ''I do find competitive sports so invigorating. But you must call me Leda, now that we're all going to be teammates.''

''I don't play,'' Gwen said as she gave the handle of the pasta machine another crank. She couldn't believe it. Cool sophisticated Leda Thatcher had turned perky overnight—and she had gone so far as to join Robert Beltramo's basketball team. Gwen didn't even want to think about what had happened over dinner at Leda's house last evening. Bad enough that she'd stayed awake until at least two in the morning stewing and steaming about it.

''Listen, Ms....uh, Leda. I'm sure Robert wouldn't mind if you went and knocked on the office door. I'm very busy—''

''Oh, no, no, I won't disturb him. And I won't keep you long, Gwennie. Just give dear Roberto a message for me. Tell him I can't *possibly* thank him enough for what he did last night. It was just...extraordinary. There's no other word for it.'' Now Leda's face didn't merely glow; it seemed positively luminescent. ''It's a night I will remember the rest of my life, and all because of Roberto Beltramo! You will tell him, won't you?''

At this point, Gwen was on the verge of tossing the pasta machine right through the window. She controlled herself only for the sake of the cheerful reindeer decorating the windowpane. Horrified at the possibility that Leda would share more details about her "extraordinary" evening, Gwen quickly brought the conversation to an end.

"All right, I'll give *Roberto* your message—verbatim. But I really have to get back to work."

"Of course. I can tell the dear boy is busy, too, and I don't want to disrupt his schedule." Leda moved toward the door, then stopped. "My, I almost forgot. I came to give you and Roberto an advance copy of my review. It will be in the newspaper tomorrow, and I'm sure you'll both be pleased with it." Leda took a folded sheet of paper from her purse, laid it on the counter and then floated out of the kitchen. "Toodle-oo!"

Toodle-oo, indeed. Gwen stared at that sheet of paper, wanting to shred it into little pieces. She wished she'd never come up with the idea of bringing a food critic to Pop's Restaurant. Now Robert Beltramo had turned into "the dear boy," and Leda Thatcher would be the one bouncing a ball on the basketball court with him. Gwen had never felt more out of sorts in her life. At last she picked up the sheet of paper, snapped it open and rapidly scanned the typescript.

Leda had written a resplendent review, praising both Gwen and Robert lavishly. Gwen's white fish with rosemary was "exquisite," her truffle soup "splendid." Robert's sardines with orange sauce were "superb," his honey ice cream "delectable." Leda finished up by urging all her readers to hurry at once to Pop's Restaurant on the River Walk, "where you will be hard pressed to choose between Gwen Ferris's informal, relaxed tea-parlor atmosphere and Robert Beltramo's brisk, no-nonsense approach to the business of eating. Either way, dear readers, your taste buds will delight to a savory feast."

Gwen slapped the review back down on the counter. This wasn't right; it wasn't right at all. First off, Leda Thatcher was not known for exuberant praise. In the past, if she'd decided that a restaurant served "adequate fare," that was a high accolade from her. In this review, Leda sounded like a mush-brain! Eating Robert's late-night dinner had obviously impaired her judgment—severely impaired it. At this rate, the woman would soon be extolling the taste of straw. Darn it, Gwen had wanted a review that really meant something—not one based on Robert Beltramo's ability to charm the woman!

Gwen sank onto a stool and propped her elbows wearily on the counter. Every minute it seemed to her that the pressure in her life was growing more and more intense until it threatened to overwhelm her, and all because of Robert Beltramo. Before she'd met him, she'd had the restaurant completely and happily under control, providing both herself and her customers with a relaxed congenial atmosphere. She'd also been cheerfully settled into a relaxed engagement that was marred by only a few vague doubts—doubts she'd been sure she could resolve. These days, however, her restaurant was a prize in a no-holds-barred power struggle and her doubts about her engagement had escalated to detonation level. Sometimes she felt as if she was hanging on desperately to a stick of dynamite, trying everything she could to keep Robert from lighting the fuse. Just when she'd thought matters couldn't get any worse, it turned out that Robert and Leda had shared an "extraordinary" evening together, and Gwen was consumed by the most appalling jealousy. What else could go wrong?

Gwen jumped up from her stool and started banging some pots around defiantly. She was about to do something drastic with her meat mallet when Robert came striding into the kitchen carrying a large box.

"Lord, Gwendolyn, do you have to make such a racket? You sound like a drummer in a heavy metal band."

Robert plunked the box on a counter and started extracting items from it: paper plates, paper napkins, paper cups, paper place mats, even paper bowls. They were decorated with colorful Christmas designs—impressionistic renderings of candles, wreaths and bells, all drawn with bold slanting lines. Still swinging her mallet, Gwen went to pick up one of the cups. The slanting red candles all around the rim looked as if they were trying to run a race with each other. Action, motion—the designs personified Robert far more than they did the gentle spirit of Christmas. Gwen set the cup down disdainfully.

"You actually think these throwaway plates and all will put your customers in the holiday mood?"

"They'll do the trick. And they're fully recyclable. Nothing throwaway about 'em."

"Christmas is for heirlooms passed down from generation to generation. Decorations you unpack and use again and again, year after year. It's about family traditions, not about paper cups!" Gwen waved her mallet for emphasis and Robert gave her a quizzical look.

"You seem mighty worked up about a couple of innocent cups and paper plates. What's the real story, Gwendolyn?"

She drew a deep breath to calm herself. It didn't do any good; she still felt like a pressure cooker about to blow its lid. There was nothing for it but to snatch up Leda's review and thrust it under Robert's nose.

"Take a look at this. Just take a look."

He smoothed out the sheet of paper and read it, a grin slowly transforming his face. "What do you know. Leda was impressed with the two of us, very impressed."

"She was impressed with *you*," Gwen retorted. "After you fed her sardines and ice cream last night, she apparently lost all her common sense. It's pathetic. She was just in here, going on and on about what a 'dear boy' you were, and how grateful she was that you'd provided her with the most 'extraordinary' evening of her life."

Robert had the perversity to look startled. "She called it extraordinary?"

Gwen frowned at a paper place mat decorated with modernistic silver bells. If those bells could ring, she knew they'd make only a dissonant jangle. "That's right, Leda said the evening was extraordinary. She wanted to make absolutely sure I told you that. She said she couldn't possibly thank you enough for last night. What on earth did you feed her, Beltramo?''

He began to chuckle in a most infuriating fashion. Gwen scowled at him.

"You want to share the joke, R.B.? I don't know if you realize what a state Leda's in. It's not exactly a laughing matter. The poor woman was even wearing one of your basketball jerseys."

Robert held up one of his paper cups and turned it around in one hand as if examining the finest crystal. "Would you say Leda seemed happy?"

"Too happy, if you ask me," Gwen muttered. "Here's a woman notorious for being snooty, but today she's decided we're all going to be the best of friends. I'm telling you, Robert, you've had a very disturbing effect on this woman. Would you please stop laughing about it?"

"I'm happy, too, Gwennie, that's all. Last night's dinner with Leda was even more of a success than I could've hoped." He started to whistle the music to an Italian love song, clearly satisfied with himself. Gwen knew she couldn't tolerate much more. She took the place mat decorated with bells and started folding it with a sense of purpose—a crease here, a tuck there.

"If you think you're a success because you made Leda babble about your cooking, well, you're wrong. All this review means is that Leda's gone dotty and it's your fault. She's serious about you. I just hope you're serious, too."

Robert studied Gwen across the counter. "Are you saying you want me to date Leda Thatcher? On a long-term basis, not just as a one-night sort of thing?"

Gwen flushed. Truth was, she hoped fervently that Robert would never so much as look at Leda Thatcher again. But she couldn't very well say that. She wasn't supposed to feel this way—so miserable and jealous her skin would probably start turning green any minute.

"As far as Leda's concerned, well, she's gone romantic, that's what it is. Nothing's worse for a woman than going romantic. It means her judgment disappears down the drain and she'll probably end up getting hurt. I'd hate to see you hurt Leda. That's what I'm saying."

Robert nodded thoughtfully. "So what you have here is just some altruistic concern for Leda's welfare. No personal interest in the matter?"

"You keep forgetting I'm engaged, Beltramo. It's not up to me to have any personal interest in your love life. That's the last thing I should have any interest in!" Gwen gave the place mat one final decisive crease and held up the paper airplane she'd created. She aimed it across the room and watched with satisfaction as it skimmed the air and landed on top of a pizza oven.

Robert watched the plane's trajectory, too, with a critical expression. Then he started folding a place mat of his own, this one decorated with energetic wreaths of holly. "Guess I'll have to let you in on a secret. I didn't serve dinner to Leda Thatcher last night."

Gwen shook her head. "Give me a break. She was in here just a little while ago, telling me all about your evening together. I know you cooked dinner for her."

"But I didn't serve it. I had Jeremy pack some of my food up, and then I had him deliver it to her house. That's what he was busy doing while you and I were out playing basketball. I didn't even see Leda last night."

Gwen stared at him. "You mean, when Leda talked about the 'dear boy'—she meant Jeremy? And Jeremy's the one who inducted her into the Beltramo Buccaneers?"

Robert's grin widened as he made an elaborate crease in his place mat. "Sounds like it. Sounds like the two of them had a fine time together, all around. And I didn't even know I had matchmaking potential."

Gwen sank back down onto the stool, the relief flooding over her making her feel positively weak-kneed. Robert hadn't spent the evening with Leda Thatcher. Gwen almost smiled, but then all sorts of disturbing implications came crowding in on her. The very intensity of her relief was alarming. She straightened up and tightened the knot on her apron strings with a yank.

"This is worse than ever," she muttered. "Leda Thatcher and Jeremy! He's only twenty...."

"Almost twenty-one," Robert said as he went on folding the place mat. "Jeremy's not a kid, even though you like to think of him as your little brother. He can handle himself, and so can Leda."

"She came in here all lit up like a Christmas tree. It was scary. Really, it was. If she's like that after one evening of romance, what's going to happen next? And why on earth did you let me go on thinking it was *you* and Leda?"

"Because that's what you wanted to believe. You wanted to think the worst about me—that I'd actually use an evening with Leda just to get a decent review for my side of the restaurant. You don't want to believe anything good about me. And you sure don't want to admit there's anything good about romance. You're engaged to the most unromantic guy around, and you want to keep yourself safe that way."

He held up his own paper airplane. Lean and streamlined, it whizzed through the air to land on top of a refrigerator—several feet farther along than Gwen's plane. She stared at it in exasperation.

"It's not about keeping myself safe. It's about choosing something that will last, just like I choose plates made out of china, instead of paper."

"Are you sure old Scott's the one who can give you china plates, Gwennie? Are you positive he's the one? Think about it." Laughter skimmed Robert's voice, light as the whisper of a paper airplane on the air. And Gwen knew she was in deeper trouble than ever— deeper doubt about Scott and deeper confusion about Robert Beltramo. Robert was a man who would never give her an inch. He played to win, whether the game was basketball or paper airplanes or the restaurant Gwen loved. Yet, even knowing this, part of her still exulted because he hadn't shared an intimate evening with Leda Thatcher. And along with the exultation came all sorts of new and dissatisfied longings, desires surely too poignant ever to find fulfillment.

Gwen retreated at last to her own side of the kitchen. She had to remember that Scott would never make her feel these wild painful longings. She had to remember that, or she'd be lost forever. Almost frantically she poured flour into a bowl. She tried to concentrate only on her dinner menu of gnocchi dumplings and stuffed mushroom caps and cheese pie.

She tried very hard not to listen as Robert whistled the soulful romantic music of Italy.

CHAPTER TEN

JEREMY AND LEDA were in love. Little more than twenty-four hours after they'd first laid eyes on each other, they were in love. Anybody could see it, even Gwen, who didn't *want* to see it. That evening Leda came to eat dinner at the restaurant just so she could sit on Robert's side and have Jeremy serve her. As Jeremy poured Leda's wine, he gazed at her raptly. As Leda nibbled her pasta, she gazed back at him, bedazzled. Aristocratic food critic Leda Thatcher, falling madly in love with a waiter—you couldn't get much more romantic than that. Gwen peered out at the besotted couple a few times, telling herself it was disgust she felt, not envy. She almost convinced herself.

Leda stayed on until the restaurant closed, but at last she and Jeremy went off together arm in arm. Claudine left, too, and only Gwen and Robert remained to close up. They both walked out the front door at the same time, and Gwen turned to lock up.

"Good night, Robert. I hope you're satisfied with the monster you've created. Jeremy was so moony-eyed he kept waiting on Leda's table and nobody else's."

Robert didn't seem disturbed. "You have to make allowances for this type of thing. Sometimes romance is more important than the ordinary practical details of running a restaurant."

"Right. I'm sure you really believe that." Gwen began striding down the River Walk toward home, but Robert caught up to her and inexorably steered her in the opposite direction.

"Let me show you something tonight, Gwennie. Remember, you owe me a favor for finding your ring."

"I don't owe you anything, Beltramo."

"Yes, you do. I found your ring twice. After the last time, you promised you'd go on a date with me."

She resisted the pull of his hand. "I did not promise a date. I'm not about to go anywhere with you. The whole point of your finding my ring was so I could put it back on and stay engaged to Scott—"

"All right, this isn't a date, then. It's a business meeting. Our long-delayed partnership meeting on the Paseo del Rio." He tucked her hand into the crook of his elbow, too much like the way Jeremy had escorted Leda earlier that evening. Gwen tried to wiggle her hands free, but Robert wouldn't let go.

"If you have something you need to show me, just show me," she said. "Let's get it over with."

"Patience, Gwendolyn. Our partnership meeting hasn't even started yet. And I'm sure Scott will understand that two business partners need to hold a meeting now and then."

Gwen suspected that placid Scott wouldn't mind how many partnership meetings she held, as long as he could expect some of her minestrone soup and *focac-*

cia bread when he came back into town. But that was beside the point.

"Robert, what do you want from me? You're already trying to take over my restaurant. Can't you leave my personal life alone?"

"Not when *you're* left alone on a beautiful December night. Old Scott's not here with you, but I am." He drew her on toward the shops and restaurants of the River Walk. Here below street level was a carefree enchanting world all its own. The joyfulness of San Antonio spilled around them in the cool night air: laughter and happy talk and Spanish love songs. More romantic music—that was dangerous. Gwen began to feel like she was out for an amorous stroll with her *novio*.

"*Novio,* indeed," she said under her breath, her fingers curling on Robert's arm.

"What was that?" he asked. "You say you wish I was your *novio?* Now that's a tantalizing idea."

Robert gave the Spanish a sensuous appealing accent, just as when he spoke Italian. At last Gwen slipped her hand away from him.

"I already have a fiancé, remember?"

Robert put his arm around her and drew her close again. "I'm starting to think you have a fiancé in name only. Look at it this way. Being a fiancé is a job like any other. You have to work at it, you have to put in the hours. Old Scott pays a lot more attention to selling computer programs than he does to you. Maybe you need someone else to take over—someone who can do the job right."

He was teasing her again. She knew it, but she had a very difficult time being flippant in return. She couldn't think straight with Robert's arm draped around her shoulders so cozily.

"I've had boyfriends who do all that courtship flummery. Candlelight dinners and flowers, moony talk and all the rest of it. Never means anything. Never means someone's going to stick by you when things get tough."

"Gwennie," Robert murmured, his arm tightening around her. "You're giving up too soon. You haven't known real flummery. Give me a chance. I can provide you with genuine flummery—"

"I should know better. I should know better than to ever open my mouth around you!"

"I can tell that what you need is food. That's the first step—that'll soften you up." He steered her toward a Mexican restaurant that was still open, and before she knew it she was seated at a small patio table, a menu spread in front of her.

She couldn't concentrate on the menu. Instead, she stared across at Robert.

"I know what you're up to," she said grimly. "This whole ridiculous situation with Jeremy and Leda has given you ideas. You think you can prove to me that I really am susceptible to romance. It won't work, Robert. I look at Jeremy and Leda, and I just wonder how long it'll take for all their romantic illusions to come crashing down to reality. And I'm finally wise enough to be suspicious about my own illusions."

"You're a hardened case, Gwennie. But at least you're willing to admit you have illusions."

Oh, she had them, all right. But "delusions" might be a better word. Already she'd caught herself musing about sunlit hours in Italy with a dark-haired man beside her, a man who was always ready to laugh and who teased her relentlessly....

Gwen twisted the ring on her finger round and round. She was being very affected by Leda and Jeremy, that was the problem. Romance had permeated the restaurant all day, rather like an infectious miasma. Combined with the fact that Gwen had hardly taken time to eat, no wonder she felt a little lightheaded. Maybe some food *would* be a good idea.

She ordered hot peppers stuffed with cheese and fried in a tasty batter. It seemed like a very long time since she'd simply sat back and enjoyed a complete meal cooked by someone else. When the food came, neither she nor Robert spoke. He was busy with his own plate of enchiladas. As chefs, they both knew that good food deserved proper concentration.

Gwen ate the last bite of her rellenos, giving a sigh of contentment as she broke open a piece of cornbread. Then she realized Robert was watching her with an amused expression.

"I know what you're thinking, Beltramo. You're thinking that Scott never takes me out to eat. But, you know, I'm perfectly capable of going to a restaurant on my own to enjoy a good meal. I don't need a man for that."

Robert sipped his beer. "Your fiancé's no good for vacations in Italy or meals in restaurants. He's never around to take you on a date, so if you want to have any fun, you might as well do it on your own. Basically, we could say old Scott is known more for his *non*presence than anything else. What real use is he, then?''

"Dammit! He's not a kitchen utensil. He doesn't have to be of use. He just has to be steady and dependable.''

"Dependable. Boring's more like it,'' Robert murmured.

Gwen knew this conversation was headed nowhere good. She set down her uneaten cornbread and glanced at her watch with determination. "Thanks for dinner, Robert, but it's time for me to go home.''

"You're not getting off that easily. I still have something to show you.'' He escorted her from the restaurant and onto one of the wide flat boats that toured the river. Each boat had its own name—*Carmela* or *Analicia* or *Rosa Linda*. Robert chose a boat painted bright red and named *Maria Elena*. A few other passengers were aboard, and Robert led Gwen to secluded seats on one of the benches. As the boat chugged slowly along, the jocular young captain pointed out the sights and made jokes that soon had the other passengers laughing in delight. But to Gwen it seemed that she and Robert were lost in their own private world. Robert's voice was low and husky when he spoke next.

"Tell me what you see, Gwennie. Tell me if you see the magic.''

She held her arms tightly against her body, as if that would help her resist the seductiveness of his words. Holiday lights draped every tree, casting a shimmer of red, blue and green onto the water. Hundreds of glimmering Christmas luminarias lined the River Walk. Each was a small paper bag filled with sand and turned into a lovely, whimsical lantern by a lighted candle inside. And so there was light everywhere in the darkness, a glittering wonderland through which the boat glided gently. It seemed to Gwen that all the stars had scattered to earth, caught in the branches of the trees or strewn along the banks of the river. She sat beside Robert and knew somehow that they both shared the same fanciful vision. Still hugging her arms against her body, she listened to the sound of her own heartbeat. A dangerous knowledge hovered on the edge of her consciousness, and she resisted it with all her strength. She didn't want to admit what was happening to her this dazzling night....

Gwen was trembling with strange new emotions by the time the boat docked and Robert helped her onto the sidewalk. She had to get away from him, that was all she knew. But he took her hand, not allowing her to escape.

"Gwendolyn, I don't know if that boat ride did the job. You still want to get away from me. I can tell that I'll have to work a little harder with you. I have to step up the flummery, and I know just how to do it." Once again he was teasing her, his way of putting distance between them. Gwen suspected that perhaps the Christmas magic of the river had touched him, too, and he was pulling back in his own fashion.

He squired her into a country-western bar, where a sultry waltz was playing. Robert took her right to the dance floor and put his arm around her, resting his cheek against her hair. He danced shamelessly close to her, humming the music in her ear, his hand moving over her back. She felt the rough-soft skin of his cheek against hers, and she knew he was planning on kissing her right there on the dance floor. He'd kiss her, and the laughter would never stop sparkling in his eyes.

Gwen drew back from Robert, staring at him. Yes, she saw the humor in his expression. When matters threatened to get too serious between them, he would always be ready with another joke. In his own way he knew how to keep Gwen at a distance—oh, he knew, all right. But even realizing this didn't keep her from finally admitting the truth.

She was starting to fall in love with Robert Beltramo. Against all her better judgment and common sense, she was falling hard. And she feared it was already too late to stop herself.

Gwen turned and fled from the bar. She ran from Robert as if her life depended on it, leaving the music and chatter behind. She didn't slow down, not until she reached the quieter, residential section of the River Walk. Even here holiday lights were aglow. The cool air made her shiver and she rubbed her arms. She gazed into the river, not surprised when she heard footsteps approaching. It was the sound of Robert's cowboy boots on the stone path. He stopped behind her.

"It's gone too far now," she said quietly without looking at him. "You know it has, Robert. You can try to joke about it, or whatever you like, but it's gone too far."

He didn't answer, and at last Gwen swiveled around. In the shadows Robert's expression was tight, impassive, as if he'd shuttered all his feelings away.

"What do you want from me?" she asked. "I know you like a good fight, and I'm sure giving you one heck of a fight over the restaurant. But as far as the rest of it...what do you want from me?"

He moved restlessly along the riverbank. "Maybe you've been right all along. Maybe I'm just making your life difficult so I won't have to face my own demons."

Gwen ached inside. She knew that if Robert had said one word to her about love, only one word, she would have yanked the engagement ring off her finger and tossed it away forever. The measure of her foolishness was that she could even *hope* for such a word from Robert Beltramo.

She gazed at him in the soft flickering light of the luminarias. "You do have demons. I think they all lead back to whatever happened between you and your father. Find out what they are, dammit. And give *me* a chance to find out if I still have anything left with Scott. At least give me that chance."

He stared back at her, his features still impassive. "You've always had your chance. I'm not stopping you from making the choice you want. A safe predictable life with a guy who can't hurt you because neither one of you will ever care enough about each other."

"Maybe you want to be safe, too, Robert! Maybe barreling after all your plans and goals keeps you from

feeling things you don't want to feel—about Pop, and
even about me.''

Gwen turned and left the River Walk to reach her
house. And Robert let her go. This time he didn't even
try to follow.

IT WAS THE TWENTY-FOURTH of December. The
morning had dawned bright and sunny, and the sky
outside the kitchen windows was as clear and deep as
the blue enamel of Gwen's antique brooch. She fingered the brooch thoughtfully. Usually her old jewelry gave her comfort, reminding her that so much of
the past had endured and would continue to endure.
But now it was the immediate future that concerned
her the most. Tonight was Christmas Eve. Tonight the
fate of Pop's Restaurant would be decided once and
for all. Tonight Scott would come back to town, and
Gwen would decide her own fate. Never had one evening loomed so ominously.

Gwen stirred the batter for a ricotta cake and
glanced over at Robert's side of the kitchen. He should
have been here by now; the first breakfast customers
were already trickling into the restaurant. Jeremy had
called Robert's house twice, but there hadn't been an
answer either time. Where *was* he?

Gwen knew she ought to be glad for any respite
from his presence. After that evening on the River
Walk, their relationship had become more strained
than ever. Robert had stopped teasing her, allowing a
formal distance to grow between the two of them. It
had gotten to the point where she actually missed his
teasing. And all along she struggled against loving

him. She told herself she couldn't possibly allow herself to love him. It would only bring her heartache; it would only bring her unfulfilled dreams. Robert wanted to take away her restaurant. He wanted the pleasure of defeating her in this crazy contest of theirs—and when the contest was over, everything else would be over between them, too. It would be over no matter which one of them won control of the restaurant.

Gwen felt a heaviness inside her, in spite of this beautiful holiday morning. And she couldn't help feeling worried about Robert, too. He was never late for work. She slipped the ricotta cake into the oven and went to call his house for herself. Still no answer.

Without Robert, the breakfast rush turned the place into a madhouse. Gwen did her best to keep omelets zinging to customers on both sides, but she quickly ran out of fig tarts and polenta. Jeremy and Claudine scurried everywhere, no longer paying attention to any boundaries as they struggled to keep every customer happy. Then Jeremy summoned Leda's help, and the woman showed up in the kitchen to don an apron. Aristocratic Leda Thatcher, cheerfully whipping up eggs and grating cheese at Gwen's command, even stacking plates in the dishwasher when needed. Apparently, thought Gwen, it was true that love could work wonders.

With Leda's help, they managed to get through the breakfast crunch. The only thing Gwen found truly disconcerting was hearing her nickname echo throughout the restaurant. "Where do you want me to put the cake racks, Gwennie?" asked Leda. "Two more asparagus omelets, Gwennie!'' exclaimed Claudine. "More fruit plates, Gwennie," said Jeremy, who had started enunciating perfectly the moment he met Leda. Even one of the customers poked his head into the kitchen and said, "That sure was good raisin bread, Gwennie!" Hearing her nickname over and over, Gwen began to feel that Robert was present in spirit, if not in body. But what on earth had happened to him? Why hadn't he shown up yet?

As the midmorning lull set in, Gwen could no longer deny that she was very worried about Robert. She hung up her splattered apron and set out for his house almost at a jog.

She hadn't been back to Pop's house since the old man's death, and she hesitated for a moment on the path leading up to it. For the first time she realized what a gloomy place it was. The square patch of lawn was uninspired, no trees or shrubs to grace its borders—no garden at all. The wooden clapboard was painted a dismal gray; the curtains hanging at the windows were pale and limp, all the starch gone out of them. The overall impression was one of listlessness, as if the house managed to shuffle out of bed every morning but was never able to accomplish much else. No surroundings could have been less suited to Robert's dynamic personality, and Gwen understood why he'd been so eager to get away as a kid.

She went up the walk and knocked on the door. Just as when she'd tried telephoning, there was no answer. Frustrated and more worried than ever, Gwen jiggled the knob. The door wasn't locked and she was able to step inside.

"Robert?" she called softly. "Robert, are you here?" She went through the living room, scanning the boxy sofa and chairs. There were no paintings on the walls; the place had the air of a drab motel.

Gwen went across the hall to the equally colorless den—and here, at last, was Robert, sitting at Pop's old desk with a jumble of photographs spread out in front of him. He looked up at Gwen, fatigue showing on his face. This was something new to her. She was used to Robert being energetic and full of life, no matter what the circumstances. But she was very glad to see him, and the gladness caught her off balance. She stood in the doorway to the den, not quite knowing what to do next.

"We tried calling," she said. "When you didn't answer, I got—we all got—concerned. Has something happened, Robert? Is something wrong?"

He rubbed his forehead as if to clear his thoughts. "I've been taking your advice, Gwennie, that's all. Confronting those demons of mine. Damn, you don't ask for anything easy, do you?" This time the mockery in his tone was unsuccessful, and he appeared to realize it. He sat back in his chair, staring down at the photographs in front of him. "I found these last night," he said, his voice weary. "Make that the middle of the night. I couldn't sleep, and I decided to start sorting through my father's things again. These pictures were crammed behind an old suitcase upstairs— that's why I never found them before. I almost wish I hadn't found them this time. They stir up too much of the past."

Gwen moved quietly to his side and picked up one of the yellowed photographs. A pretty, dark-haired woman smiled back at her from some long-ago day, a woman whose vibrant features looked very much like Robert's.

"Your mother," Gwen murmured. "Pop kept photographs of her."

"It was a whole packet of them, tied up with a string. Not just pictures of her, but pictures of him, and me when I was a kid. Right up until I was five, the year my mother died. After that, no photographs. It's like we all stopped existing at the same time." Robert seemed to be talking to himself more than to Gwen. He stood abruptly and went to stare out the window, as if once again plotting his escape from this dreary house.

Gwen sifted through the photographs on the desk. Here was a picture of Robert's mother, laughing as she tried to hold a squirming curly-haired infant in her lap. The child had to be Robert, of course, full of action and motion from the very beginning. Another photograph showed him as a toddler, taking wobbly steps with a determined look on his face. And in another photo he was older, perhaps four or so, swinging from a set of monkey bars. The camera had carefully chronicled his first few years, but, indeed, there were no pictures of Robert as an older boy, or as a teenager who had loved basketball.

Gwen lingered over a photograph of a young Pop and his wife. They stood together in front of the restaurant, arms around each other, both wearing tall chef's hats cocked at debonair angles. They weren't looking into the camera but, instead, were smiling rather foolishly at each other. In all the time Gwen had known Pop, she'd never seen an expression like that on his face—an expression of wonder, like a man who couldn't quite believe his own good fortune and happiness.

"He loved your mother," Gwen said, brushing her fingers over the photograph. "It must have hurt him terribly when she died."

"He wouldn't talk about it. He never talked about her. I don't remember much about her, either. I only know that her name was Annetta, and that my father met her on a trip to Italy. I know he brought her back here, and they started the restaurant. They ran the place together until she died of heart disease. Sometimes it seemed he was so angry at her for dying he could never forgive her. And I think he couldn't forgive himself, or even me, for going on with life after she'd died."

Robert didn't say anything more for a long while. And Gwen didn't say anything, either. She merely sat down in front of the desk, doing one of the things she did best—listening. She listened to the charged silence in the room and waited for the words that surely had to come. And at last Robert spoke again.

CHAPTER ELEVEN

"WHEN I WENT AWAY to college, my father told me he wouldn't pay any of my expenses," Robert said quietly. "He told me he'd only help out if I stayed in San Antonio and went to school here. But I couldn't do that. I couldn't stay and become as bitter and negative as he was. I knew that was what he wanted, somebody to share his bitterness about the injustice of my mother's death. I just couldn't do it, dammit. I would've given anything to bring her back again—but I couldn't sour her memory with that much anger, the way he did. So I took a bus to Austin and got myself a job working in a restaurant. That's how I put myself through school. Made the old man madder than ever. There I was, cooking pasta in somebody else's joint, instead of his."

Robert jammed his hands into the pockets of his jeans. He paced restlessly over the grayish carpet of the den, and now he spoke quickly, as if anxious to get out words that had been festering inside him too long.

"The summer after I graduated from college, I came home again. Being away had been good for me—it helped me look at my father with more compassion. So I came back that summer to see if we could be a real father and son for once. I worked in the restaurant with him every day, I went home with him every night. I tried to get him to talk about my mother. Lord, I tried to get him to talk about anything. It took three whole months of his unrelenting foul temper to finally wear me down—to make me realize the truth."

Robert stopped. He paused in the middle of the room, and he didn't speak. But Gwen knew he would have to go on; he'd have to finish what he had started. She gazed at the yellowed photographs of Robert's laughing dark-haired mother, and she wished suddenly that she could have known that woman—Annetta, Robert had called her. What a lovely name. Annetta.

At last Robert did go on, his voice so low that Gwen had to strain to hear him. "I finally realized that too much of my father had died right along with my mother. The only way he wanted me around was if I'd consent to die inside, too. He hated all the efforts I made to cheer him up that summer. He finally told me to get the hell out—but that's not why I left. I left because his bitterness was starting to get to me—starting to get inside me. I could feel it coloring the way I looked at things and how I remembered my mother. It scared me, thinking I could really become like my father. So I left, Gwennie, and I never came back. I went to New York, because that was about as far away as I could go. Sure, I wrote letters to my dad, but he never answered them. In a way I was relieved he didn't answer. Whenever I called him on the phone, he always found an excuse to hang up fast. And that was a relief, too. The time between my letters and phone calls just got longer and longer, and then I found out that he'd died. I never even knew he was sick.''

Gwen stared down at the photograph of Pop Beltramo and Annetta, the woman he'd loved. Everything would have been so different for him if she had lived; he hadn't been strong enough to survive graciously without her. It struck Gwen that this was what Pop had always lacked: a fundamental graciousness toward life and toward other human beings that perhaps only his wife could have given him.

Gwen stood up and went to Robert. "You really did come back to San Antonio to make peace with your dad. To realize that he loved you, in spite of everything.''

"I don't know," Robert said. "I don't know why the hell I came back." He picked up an old battered cowboy hat of black felt and turned it around in his hands. "I left this behind when I went to New York all those years ago. Guess I left a lot of things behind— I've been going through the house, finding traces of my life where I didn't expect them. This hat, my old boots—every day seems like I find something else I'd forgotten about.''

A realization struck Gwen. She could see everything clearly now. Somehow she had to make Robert see, too. "Then all the clues are here in this house. The way you've kept finding your old things around—your cowboy hat, the boots you used to wear. And then these photographs. They're all signs that Pop loved you, as well as your mother. Don't you understand?'' She gestured earnestly, needing badly to get through to him. "When you came to my house that first night,

Robert, you asked me why I didn't have any photographs of Scott, any traces of him. Because you knew that when people love someone, they keep traces around to remind them of their love. Well, that's what Pop had right here. Traces of you all over the place. I bet if you kept looking, you'd even find the letters you sent him—crammed into a corner somewhere, hidden just like the photographs.''

Robert turned away from her, toward the window again, and she couldn't tell how much of what she said he was listening to. She took a deep breath.

"There's something else, Robert, something I haven't wanted to admit. Maybe your father was talking about selling the entire restaurant to me, but the truth is, I don't think he really wanted to. He kept stalling. I think, deep down, he wanted you to have at least a part of the place as your inheritance. A proof that he loved you, perhaps. Because after your mother died, he just never had the words to tell you so. Leaving you the restaurant... I have a feeling that was his way to show you his love. I *know* it was."

"Come off it, Gwennie. You've been telling me all along my father meant you to have the place. You can't suddenly change the past because you want it to have a different ending."

Gwen almost reached up to shake Robert by the shoulders, as if that way she could shake the truth into him. "I'm not changing the past! I'm finally seeing it the way it was. No—I'm *listening* to it for the first time. I'm thinking back and listening to all the unspoken things I should've picked up on with Pop. He kept saying he wanted me to have the entire restaurant, but he never did anything about it. He'd talk, and then he'd just look out the window the way you're doing right now. And he'd look wistful, instead of grouchy the way he usually did. My bet is that he was thinking about you, or your mom, or maybe about both of you."

"It sounds good, Gwennie. It sounds real good. Lord, I wish I could believe it, but I don't think I can. I'm starting to think maybe I was a fool to come back to San Antonio. It's too late to make peace, if that really *is* why I came back."

Gwen wanted to argue. She wanted to tell him he was a hundred percent wrong, but she knew all the arguing in the world wouldn't convince him. Now, at last, something else was very clear to her. She knew exactly what she had to do tonight, on this Christmas Eve.

She knew what she had to do to make everything turn out all right—even if, in the end, it was something that would break her heart.

IT WAS A BEAUTIFUL Christmas Eve. The luminarias glowed all along the River Walk, and holiday lights glimmered in every tree. Carolers bearing long flickering candles sang outside the restaurant, rewarded for their efforts with plates of Gwen's Sicilian chocolate cake and Robert's cinnamon cannoli. Replenished, the carolers went merrily off to sing somewhere else. Gwen left the restaurant at the same time, wishing she could share the carolers' joy and enthusiasm. But she was on her way to meet Scott, and she wasn't looking forward to the encounter. She wasn't looking forward to it at all.

A few hours later Gwen returned to the restaurant. The place was dark except for a bar of light shining out from the office. Music floated from the office, too, a low refrain of Christmas carols on the radio. That was enough to make Gwen pause; Robert usually complained about the way she kept the radio going all the time, but here he was now, playing holiday music to himself.

Gwen stood in the doorway of the office and looked at Robert. His feet were up on his desk, scuffed cowboy boots crossed at the ankle. His hat was pushed back rakishly on his head. In one hand he held the small china Santa Claus that Gwen kept perching on his computer. He was gazing at the little Santa with a rather perplexed expression, as if not quite sure what to do with it. After a moment he glanced up at Gwen.

"Didn't expect you back so soon," he said. "Thought maybe you wouldn't be back at all." His tone was conversational. It was impossible to tell one way or another whether he cared that Gwen had returned. She sat down at her desk and slapped open her account ledger.

"Christmas Eve, isn't it?" she said stiffly. "Of course I'd be here. This is the night we agreed on. The night we compare our earnings to see who ends up with the restaurant."

Robert looked her over with a thoughtful expression. "So you didn't set the wedding date, after all. Good for you, Gwennie. Good for you."

She bent over her account book, rapidly jotting down a few last figures. "What makes you think I didn't set the date?" she asked. "For all you know, I'm getting married at sunup on New Year's Day!"

"You're not wearing his ring anymore. It's gone. Unless you lost it between the floorboards again, that means you gave the bruiser back to old Scott."

Gwen sighed and set down her pencil. It was no use trying to protect herself from Robert. He always saw too much, knew too much about her. She spread out her left hand. It felt so much lighter, so much freer without that heavy diamond.

"Very well," she said quietly. "In case you're really interested, I did break off my engagement to Scott. Tonight I couldn't deny the truth any longer. I looked at him and...and I just knew I couldn't spend the rest of my life looking at him. Scott's a nice man, but he simply has no passion. All of the things you said about him, unfortunately they're true. I just didn't want to admit it before. When I told him it was over, he seemed more disappointed about losing my fettuccine than about losing me." As she spoke, Gwen looked sharply at Robert. Let him try to laugh about it, let him give her one hint of a smile, and she...

But Robert didn't laugh and he didn't smile. He gazed back at her with a serious expression. "Your ex-fiancé isn't worth a fig," he said. "Don't waste any more time thinking about him."

She gouged her pencil into one of the many nicks in the surface of her old desk. "I really wanted things to work out with Scott, you know. I wanted finally, *fi-*

nally to have made the right decision about a relationship with a man.''

''Face it, Gwennie. You can't choose a guy the way you'd choose a cantaloupe. Seems romance happens when you least expect it.''

She gouged another nick in the desk. ''Don't get any wrong ideas. This doesn't mean I believe in romance all of a sudden. I just know that it's no use trying to have a relationship without at least *some* deeper feelings.''

Now humor did sparkle in Robert's eyes. He tilted his hat back even farther. ''Gwendolyn, it sounds to me like you're in a fix here. You've decided you can't live with romance—and you can't live without it. What's the solution?''

''There isn't any solution. I figure I'll just go on like I always have, very happy on my own.''

''And Italy? You'll visit Italy on your own?''

''Of course. And I'll have a wonderful time. I'll thoroughly enjoy my own company.'' She gazed defiantly at Robert. He didn't say anything else, but his mouth gave a suspicious twitch.

Gwen bent over the account book again, trying to concentrate on adding and subtracting figures. Christmas music played softly from the radio, making her ache inside with all her unfulfilled yearnings. She hadn't told Robert everything. She hadn't told him that she'd already known this morning she would break up with Scott. She'd known it when she'd gone to Robert's house and seen him with all those yellowed photographs spread out in front of him. That was the precise moment when she'd admitted to herself that she loved him.

Yes, she loved Robert Beltramo. She loved him recklessly and completely. She loved him with all the romantic longings inside her that refused to be quelled. But Gwen feared those romantic longings would get her nowhere. Robert had put up barriers between the two of them, barriers he'd made clear could not be broached. All he wanted was to win the restaurant from her. And if she were wise, she would concentrate only on this one matter herself: the fate of Pop's Restaurant.

Gwen erased a few numbers and jotted in some more. She stared at the ledger, making sure everything was exactly as she wished. Then she pushed the ledger across to Robert.

"The time's come," she said. "Let me see *your* accounts."

He was ready with his computer printouts, but he seemed reluctant to hand them over. Swinging his feet off the desk, he sat up and frowned at his printouts for a long moment.

"Robert, I'm waiting. It's time for the end of Plan C. Let's get on with it."

He rattled the pages in his hand. "Plan C was a damn good idea. I still believe that."

"It's been a constant source of aggravation for both of us."

"Maybe that's what's so good about it. Constant aggravation keeps you on your toes. Ever think of it like that?"

Gwen couldn't take the suspense any longer. She reached over, grabbed the printouts from him and scanned them hurriedly. She drew a deep breath, then let it out again. Compared to the figures in her account book, Robert had won by a respectable margin—quite a respectable margin.

"Congratulations," she said. "You get to buy out my share of the restaurant."

He was examining her accounts with far too much interest. "Thought you would've done better than this," he muttered. "Leda's review in the newspaper was good for both of us. And that crazy idea you had actually seemed to be working—pushing a bunch of your tables together and having total strangers sit down together for a family-style meal. You packed in a lot more people that way."

Gwen shrugged. "Yes, well, it did seem to be successful. It's amazing how many people enjoy a family atmosphere with just a little encouragement. But I guess you just packed in more people than me. Like I said, Robert, congratulations." She grabbed a corner of her account book and tried to tug it away from him. He wouldn't let go.

"Did you include all the meals you catered on the riverboats? And this morning at breakfast—you should count the profits for both sides as your own, since I wasn't here. Did you do that, Gwennie?"

"Everything's in order, Robert. Everything." At last she managed to tug the ledger away from him. She clapped it shut and slid it safely into a desk drawer. She was determined not to let Robert learn the truth.

Because, truth was, she'd cooked the books. She'd done everything she could to make sure her figures came out lower than Robert's. It meant forfeiting the restaurant that meant so much to her. That hurt, but it was the way things had to be. The only way.

Loving Robert had opened her eyes at last. She'd seen his struggles to resolve his pain about his father. She'd also seen, quite simply and clearly, that he would never be able to resolve that pain unless he could take the inheritance his father had left him—this restaurant. There was no longer any doubt in Gwen's mind that Pop had meant Robert to have at least half the restaurant. It was even possible that Pop regretted selling Gwen her share of the place. In the end, his thoughts must have turned to the son he'd estranged with all his bitterness. Underneath that bitterness, surely Pop had wanted to make peace with his only son. Just as now Robert wanted to make peace with his father. If Robert spent some time in the restaurant alone with his memories, no longer distracted by his competition with Gwen, that was the best way for him to find healing. It would take a long time, perhaps, but eventually he would make peace with the past. Gwen's love for Robert told her all these things.

She pushed back her chair and stood up. "I'm glad you won," she said a bit too forcefully. "You've offered me a very generous price for my share, and I'll be able to open my own restaurant somewhere else. I'll be in control of everything from the start. I'm really looking forward to it."

"Gwennie—"

"It's over, Robert. Just let it be over, all right? That way you and I can finally get on with our lives. We won't spend all our time competing and arguing, and...and the rest of it." Tears pricked her eyes, threatening to spill over. She couldn't let Robert see her crying when she was supposed to be happy, blast it. Oh, why did she have to love him? *Why?* It hurt too much.

She turned and left him, just as she'd done that night on the dance floor. But leaving him this time was far worse. This time she knew just how very much she loved him.

ON CHRISTMAS DAY Gwen wore a Mexican fiesta skirt of vivid red, shot through with silver thread like tinsel. Her white blouse was ruffled down the front, and around her neck she wore one of her favorite pieces of antique jewelry: a necklace of tarnished silver coins, held together by a delicate latticework of silver. Even disguised by a big wraparound apron, it was a festive outfit, as befitted this joyous holiday. Gwen could only hope that she looked joyous on the outside. Inside, she was grieving. This would be her last day at the restaurant—her very last. Carrying a large bowl of cranberries, she hurried from the kitchen to the dining area, only to bump smack into Robert.

"Easy," he said, steadying her with his strong warm hands. "You've been dashing back and forth all morning like goblins are after you. Time to slow down a little."

"You have your holidays mixed up. Goblins are for Halloween, remember?" Gwen's attempt to sound

lighthearted was unsuccessful, and she brushed past
Robert. Every time she looked at him, she seemed to
add one more measure of pain to her heart. She was
starting to wish the day would be over quickly so she
could go home and wrap herself in comforting solitude. But it was only noon, and the festivities had
barely started. Today Gwen and Robert were throwing open the doors of the restaurant, offering a free
Christmas dinner to low-income families.

People crowded into the place as never before,
mingling freely from one side to the other. Gwen and
Robert offered all sorts of Christmas delicacies: tra-
ditional turkey and stuffing, creamy mashed pota-
toes, yams swimming in brown-sugar sauce, freshly
baked rolls with generous dollops of sweet butter. But
there was Italian fare, too: lasagna with pesto sauce,
peppery sausages and tomatoes simmered in olive oil,
crepes folded over a stuffing of ham and fontina
cheese to earn the nickname ''Grandma's kerchiefs.''
For dessert, pumpkin pie was served right along with
the ricotta cake and Robert's Christmas tortoni—
frosty macaroon cream garnished with brightly striped
candy canes.

Keeping food on everyone's plate turned into a
hectic job. Gwen was glad of all the distractions, but
she still found herself constantly thinking about Robert and about saying goodbye to her restaurant. Robert didn't make things any easier for her. No matter
how many holiday celebrants trooped into the restaurant, and no matter how frantically he and Gwen
cooked to keep up with the crowd's appetite, he always seemed to find time to gaze at her from his side

of the kitchen. He didn't tease her or try to joke with her; he simply watched her with that thoughtful expression of his. It rattled her so much that she almost burned an entire tray of gingerbread men.

Claudine, Jeremy and Leda were all there to pitch in and help, although Jeremy and Leda were so enthralled with each other that sometimes they forgot to keep the cranberry punch flowing along with the strawberries in wine. For Gwen, it was almost as painful to look at the happy couple as it was to look at Robert. She wondered if romance would endure for Leda and Jeremy. In spite of her downhearted spirits, she hoped so; she hoped romance could work for *someone*.

The grand finale of the celebration came late in the afternoon, when Robert hung a papier-mâché piñata from a rope in the very center of the restaurant—right between his side and Gwen's. The piñata was shaped like a plump reindeer, decorated all over with curls of red and green crepe paper, an elegant Christmas bow adorning the tip of each antler.

"Who's first?" Robert called, only to be surrounded by a swarm of excited children. Laughing, he picked the smallest child, a solemn little girl with dark pigtails. He bent to tie a bandanna around the child's eyes as a blindfold, all the while his own eyes on Gwen. She tried to look away but couldn't, her heart thumping uncomfortably. She didn't know what silent message Robert was attempting to send her. She didn't want to know; it was already difficult enough that she kept finding new qualities to admire in him. For one, he was good with children. He joked with the blindfolded little girl and soon had her grinning, her solemnity vanished. Next he turned the little girl round and round. When it seemed she was thoroughly dizzy, he gave her a wooden stick and jumped out of her way barely in time. She charged forward, brandishing her stick vigorously in search of the elusive reindeer piñata as it frolicked backward and forward along the rope.

Jeremy was the one who manned the reindeer by pulling it up and down, and he did such a good job of it that one blindfolded kid after the other was unable to attack the frisky piñata. But then Jeremy smiled moonily at Leda, forgot to pull the reindeer along, and a triumphant little boy got a good whack at it. The poor reindeer cracked wide open, spewing candies onto both sides of the restaurant. Children scrambled wildly after them . . . and once again Robert gazed intently at Gwen. Darn it, what did he want from her? Wasn't it enough that now the restaurant was finally his?

It was evening before the last guests had straggled out of the restaurant. Claudine, Jeremy and Leda stayed to help clean up, but then they departed, too, off to celebrate their own family Christmases. Gwen and Robert were left alone in the kitchen, exactly what Gwen didn't want. She untied her splattered apron and tossed it over a stool.

"I'm out of here," she said. "This is it. Merry Christmas, Robert . . . and goodbye. Good luck and . . . just goodbye."

CHAPTER TWELVE

ROBERT WOULDN'T LET her go. "You can't leave yet, Gwennie. I want you to look at something first."

Somehow she'd known this wasn't going to be an easy farewell; Robert never made anything easy for her. "Is it that important?" she asked. "Can't we just wish each other the best, and end things—"

"Wait right here. This is definitely something you need to see." He left the kitchen, returning a moment later with more of his computer printouts and Gwen's account book.

"What are you doing with all that?" she demanded. "Darn it, we settled our accounts last night."

He spread the book and the printouts on the counter. "I could tell something fishy was going on last night. Your side of the restaurant's been doing too well for you to come up with such mediocre profits. So after you left, I ran your accounts through my computer to double-check them."

"You had no right—"

"Gwennie, I have bar graphs here," he said in a tone of satisfaction. "Not to mention pie charts, box plots and frequency curves. Any way you look at it, you're the winner, not me. You brought in the most money."

"I don't believe it," Gwen muttered. "This has to be another one of your jokes." She riffled through the computer printouts, examining different figures. Robert *had* actually printed out a graph or two—very obnoxious graphs, as far as she was concerned. And if the numbers were to be believed, Gwen had made the most money during Plan C. She'd won by a narrow yet respectable margin.

She slapped down the printouts. "Robert, everything would've been just fine if you hadn't gone poking your nose into my ledger! The restaurant is supposed to be yours. I don't want it."

He propped an elbow on the counter. "I happen to know you can hardly stand the thought of leaving this place, Gwendolyn. So why'd you do it? Why'd you fudge the numbers?"

She sighed, gazing at the gingerbread house she'd finished constructing last week. She snatched a piece of red licorice that served as a border around the outside of the house and popped it into her mouth. "It's simple," she said finally. "I'm convinced Pop really wanted you to have the restaurant. And I'm convinced you'll never resolve your feelings about your dad unless you can claim the inheritance he wanted you to have. That's it. End of story."

"There's always my version of the story. Or maybe Dickens's version is the best." Robert gave a faint smile. "Last night I finished reading *A Christmas Carol*, Gwennie. I did a lot of thinking about Scrooge, and how he really did have a good heart underneath all his orneriness. And I remembered all the things you said about my father—how you believed he had a good heart, too, underneath *his* orneriness. I've decided I want to believe that about my dad. I want to believe there was as much hope for him as there was for Scrooge.''

Robert paused for a moment, then went on slowly, ''I'll never know for sure what my father was really thinking or feeling. He turned in on himself after my mother's death. He wouldn't let anyone else get through to him, except maybe you. But I look at those clues you pointed out to me, the traces of my life my father kept around. And I have to tell myself those clues mean something. I have to tell myself that he *did* care about me. And I have to believe that this Christmas my dad's with my mother somewhere, finally happy now that he's found her again.''

Gwen felt an odd tightness in her throat. ''That's a very romantic notion,'' she said. ''Pop and Annetta together again. I can't help liking it.''

''So you really *are* susceptible to romance, Gwennie. You try to be cynical, but deep down you're as bad as Leda and Jeremy.''

Gwen turned quickly away from Robert. ''I hope I'm not that much of a moon-heart,'' she grumbled. ''Surely I have a little common sense left. And we really ought to talk business, Robert. About the restaurant—''

''I have it all figured out. I have a new plan.''

Gwen swung back toward him. ''Oh, no. I don't like the sound of this, not one bit. Another one of your plans!''

Robert had that look on his face, the enthusiastic determined look that meant he was ready to overcome any obstacle to his goals. He straightened up from the counter and grinned at her.

"Damn, this is a good plan. The best so far. Plan G, that's what it is."

Gwen surveyed him doubtfully. "Shouldn't it be Plan D? We just got finished with Plan C, after all."

"No, this is Plan G. G, as in Gwendolyn. As in Gwennie. And this is how it'll work. You and I will keep running the restaurant together, just the way we've been doing. We'll keep on competing and arguing and driving each other nuts. And we'll do it for fifty years or so. Make that seventy or eighty years. Because I've never had so much fun as when I'm with you. I wake up every morning inventing new Italian fast foods that'll make you crazy, and I want to keep doing that the rest of my life. What do you say? Will you agree to Plan G? You'd better say yes, Gwennie, because I love you."

He came around the counter toward her, and without another thought Gwen went straight into his arms. At last the holiday joy she'd been missing swept through her. It made her feel positively bedazzled, as if all the shimmering lights of the River Walk now belonged only to her.

"I must be a moon-heart, after all," she said. "Because I want Plan G, too. I want to wake up every morning and try to figure out how I'm going to mess up your side of the kitchen. I want to wake up every morning—and kiss you like this...."

It was a very long while before Robert and Gwen broke apart. When they did, they were both breathing unevenly and had to cling to each other for support. But then Robert dug into the pocket of his jeans and brought out a small box wrapped in gold foil.

"Your Christmas present, Gwennie. You've already given me the best gift I've ever had—a peacefulness about my father. Now I want you to have this."

Fingers trembling, Gwen peeled back the wrapping paper to reveal a velvet jewelry box. She opened the hinged lid, catching her breath at what she saw inside.

A ring. A perfect ring, a simple stone of rich creamy jade set in age-burnished gold. It wasn't flashy or showy in the least; instead, it possessed a unique subtle beauty. Gwen ran a finger over the curve of the stone.

"Oh, Robert . . ."

"I kept seeing it in a window of an antique store along the River Walk. I kept going back and looking at it, thinking how much more it suited you than that monster diamond you wore. I bought the ring a few days ago, Gwennie. I told myself it was my Christmas present for you—but now I'm hoping it can be something more." He smiled at her, his eyes a very dark amber-brown. "I realize you just got rid of one engagement ring, but if you'd consider wearing another, you'd make me very happy."

"Yes, Robert. Yes." She slipped the jade ring onto her finger. "It fits," she murmured against the soft cotton of his shirt. "It fits perfectly."

"Hey, after chasing that diamond all over creation, I ought to know what size you wear. Enough to ake a pretty good guess, anyway. But I hope you don't want to lose *this* ring, Gwennie. It's starting to mean a lot to me already.''

She wiggled the fingers of her left hand. The weight of the jade ring was just right—not too heavy at all. "This is one ring I don't need to lose," she said contentedly. "This is going to stay with me forever."

Robert ran his hand over her hair, smoothing it away from her face. His touch was warm and gentle. "It was killing me, you wearing another man's ring. The whole time, it was killing me. I just didn't want to admit it. I was pretty confused about why I'd come back to San Antonio, and I was trying to sort out my life. I didn't think I had room for any more complications. But last night, when I found out you'd finally dumped your boyfriend... You don't know how relieved I was, Gwennie. And after you walked out of here and I felt what it would be like without you—I couldn't face that. You belong here with me. This is where my real home is. With you. Only with you."

She hugged him fiercely. "I'm the one who didn't want to admit the truth. I kept telling myself I could be happy without romance. I was just plain scared of *real* romance, the kind that burst into my life right along with you. But now it's taken me over, and there's not a thing I can do about it! You'll have to come to Italy with me, Robert. That's all there is to it."

He kissed her tenderly. "We're going to have a long and exciting honeymoon in Rome and Venice and wherever else you want to go. And then we'll come home to your rabbit Whiskers, and to your house with all its possibilities...."

"Our house," Gwen amended, her happiness sure and strong. "You'd better remember to bring your tool belt with you. After all, you'll have to put up a basketball hoop as your first project. If we're going to have a team, we'll have to get in a lot of practice."

"Gwennie, are you actually saying you'll join the Buccaneers? I've finally recruited you?" That wonderful familiar humor glimmered in his eyes, but Gwen was quite solemn as she twined her fingers in his hair.

"The way I see things, there's already a jersey with my name on it in big yellow letters. Can't let that go to waste, can I? Besides, I'm sure you'll have all our kids out dribbling a ball while they're still in diapers. I have to stay in shape so I can keep up."

Robert drew her closer. "Here's what we'll do. We'll send our kids outside with the basketball, while you and I get down to some serious romance as often as possible. How's that for a plan?"

"It's the best plan you've ever come up with. The very best."

"*Ti amo,* Gwennie. I love you very much." Now his voice was low and husky.

"I love you, too, Robert," she told him. "With all my heart."

And then Robert kissed her again. The restaurant was warm and snug, chili-pepper wreaths adorning the walls and evergreen boughs gracing the doorway. Gwen and Robert were together at last—for this Christmas and all the Christmases to come.

Make Christmas a truly Romantic experience—with

HARLEQUIN ROMANCE®

Wouldn't *you* love to kiss a tall, dark Texan under the mistletoe? Gwen does, in HOME FOR CHRISTMAS by Ellen James. Share the experience!

Wouldn't *you* love to kiss a sexy New Englander on a snowy Christmas morning? Angela does, in Shannon Waverly's CHRISTMAS ANGEL. Share the experience!

Look for both of these Christmas Romance titles, available in December wherever Harlequin Books are sold.

(And don't forget that Romance novels make great gifts! Easy to buy, easy to wrap and just the right size for a stocking stuffer. *And* they make a wonderful treat when you need a break from Christmas shopping, Christmas wrapping and stuffing stockings!)

HRX

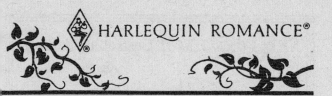

HARLEQUIN ROMANCE®

WELCOME BACK, MARGARET WAY!

After an absence of five years, Margaret Way—one of our most popular authors ever—returns to Romance!

Start the New Year with the excitement and passion of

ONE FATEFUL SUMMER
A brand-new Romance from Margaret Way

Available in January wherever Harlequin Books are sold.

HRMW

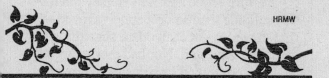

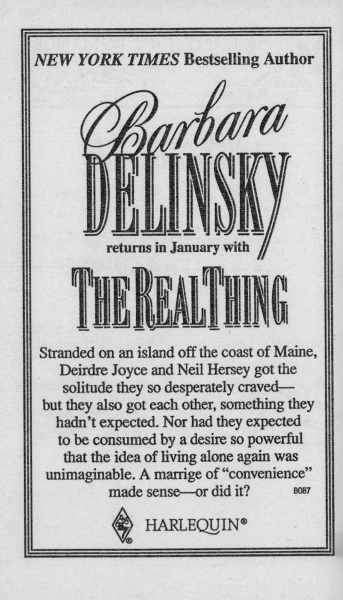

NEW YORK TIMES Bestselling Author

Barbara DELINSKY

returns in January with

THE REAL THING

Stranded on an island off the coast of Maine,
Deirdre Joyce and Neil Hersey got the
solitude they so desperately craved—
but they also got each other, something they
hadn't expected. Nor had they expected
to be consumed by a desire so powerful
that the idea of living alone again was
unimaginable. A marrige of "convenience"
made sense—or did it?

BOB7

HARLEQUIN®